# SPECIAL ED

# SPECIAL ED

## A SUPERNATURAL JOURNEY INTO REALITY

## M. D. NOMBERG

ARCHWAY
PUBLISHING

Archway Publishing books may be ordered through booksellers or by contacting:

Archway Publishing
1663 Liberty Drive
Bloomington, IN 47403
www.archwaypublishing.com
1 (888) 242-5904

ISBN: 978-1-4808-6435-1 (sc)
ISBN: 978-1-4808-6434-4 (hc)
ISBN: 978-1-4808-6433-7 (e)

Library of Congress Control Number: 2018951464

Print information available on the last page.

Archway Publishing rev. date: 7/30/2018

## Dedication

I dedicate Special Ed to my mother, who passed away a few months ago. As an avid reader, gobbling up three to four books a week, she was a tough critic who read my manuscript and expressed that she enjoyed it.

For this reason, I am publishing this book in her memory. I hope, when you read my story, you will like it as much as my mother did.

## Special Thanks

I want to extend a heart-felt debt of gratitude to Sallie W. Boyles for her superb job of editing this manuscript. For over a decade, Sallie has been a tremendous help as an editor and a friend.

M.D. Nomberg

# 1

The day was lackluster yet unsettling for Miriam, who was accustomed to her predictable though peaceful Sundays with church followed by a day devoted to Paul, her beloved husband; however, instead of waking with her usual calm, she experienced a peculiar sensation that made her shiver. Something was not quite right.

To quell the feeling, Miriam nervously begged Paul to accompany her to services. He would cut off his ear for the wife that he cherished, but Paul drew the line at letting someone tell him that he was going to hell for enjoying a cold beer. He tried to talk her into lazing at home with him, but Miriam would not relinquish her morning of prayer. Though she couldn't shake the odd feeling, Miriam didn't want Paul to worry. She put on her white, linen dress, the one that Paul said made her look like an angel, and went to Sunday services alone.

Miriam tried to tell herself that her hormones were raging, causing her unfounded anxiety. But as the day wore on, physical symptoms appeared. Her abdomen felt heavy and sensitive, as if caused by something of a feminine nature. Quietly, she made up her mind to see her doctor, just to reassure herself that it was nothing.

Before daylight broke on Monday, Miriam trudged uneasily to the bathroom. The steamy water from the shower was comforting, and she let her mind roam aimlessly. What could be causing this strange mental and physical state? Paul was still asleep, and she knew that if she told him how she was feeling, he would be alarmed. Her mind raced incessantly while wondering what could be wrong. She had experienced upset stomachs before but not like this. Paul would be waking soon because the alarm was set for six thirty, and it was six twenty now.

After her shower, Miriam dragged herself to her dressing area and sat down. She put on her makeup but wasn't actually seeing her reflection in the mirror. Instead, she conjured a vision of Paul Rippington at the moment she first met him.

He was not a particularly handsome man, nor was his physique one that caused heads to turn as he entered a room. Paul Rippington was a man of average stature and weight. His dirty-blond hair was curly and cut short. The only remarkable features of Paul's were his eyes. Though an ordinary greenish brown, they could pierce right through to one's soul, which seemed to connect instantly with Miriam's. In fact, Miriam Walker fell for him the minute his presence crossed her vision. She had met the man of her dreams.

Miriam, in contrast, was a beauty. Only her height was average. Slender but curvy, she emitted a complex air of confidence and modesty. Silky, dark-brown hair and long eyelashes framed her classic goddess features, punctuated with hazel eyes and naturally red lips. When Paul first saw her, he said, "You're beautiful!" without even realizing it.

That was ten years ago, and now after four years of marriage, she was still sure that she had made the right decision. Their courtship through college and graduate school was happy and stimulating. After all, when it was right, it was right. She believed in "happily ever after," and so did Paul. To that day, they had never had a hint of an argument. Their lives were intertwined and satisfying. Though not dependent on each other, they chose to be together as often as they could.

Miriam was fine going to church alone. She knew that they would spend the rest of the day together. As it turned out, Paul took her to their favorite French restaurant for lunch. He commented that Miriam didn't have her usual appetite, but she laughed it off, saying that she wanted to keep her figure. With a wink, Paul replied that she was as beautiful as the day they had met.

As she drifted back, the reflection of her features now in focus, Miriam was amazed to realize that she had perfectly applied her cosmetics, and only a few minutes had passed. Had she relived so much in a matter of minutes? Paul was beginning to thrash about, which meant that he would be fully awake the second the alarm cried out.

Sure enough, as soon as chimes broke the silence, Paul sat up and Miriam began to pull herself together.

"Good morning, honey," she said in a cheery tone. "Did you sleep well?"

"Yes, thanks, dear. Did you?" Realizing she was fully dressed, he asked, "Why are you up so early?"

She paused for just a second and replied, "No reason. I just wanted to get a jump on the morning because I have a lot to do today." She hoped he would let this pass as sufficient but knew better.

"Like what?"

Deciding to be straightforward, she took a deep breath. "My stomach is acting up, so I wanted to make an appointment with Dr. Greene. I thought I'd call the office when it opens. I'm sure that it's nothing."

"You're not pregnant, are you, dear?" he asked as he chuckled.

"Oh!" She hadn't thought of the possibility. "I couldn't be. Or could I?" Instead of feeling thrilled, for reasons Miriam couldn't explain, she was worried.

By ten o'clock, Miriam was waiting nervously in the examination room. Instinctively, she knew that Paul had been right. Dr.

Greene entered the room with the air of arrogance common among doctors. Ronald Greene, in fact, purposely emitted self-confidence to qualm his patients' anxieties, and Miriam, clearly, was tense.

"Good morning, Mrs. Rippington." He smiled, seeing through her mask of calm.

"Good morning, Dr. Greene."

After a perfunctory exam, he said she looked fine, but he would run a few tests just to be sure. One would be for pregnancy. At the mention of the word, Miriam felt another shiver run down her spine. Was that an omen?

Somehow, she had fumbled through the rest of the day and even decided to cook a special meal for dinner. With Miriam busy in the kitchen, Paul sat down to read the paper and watch a few minutes of news. He was about to pull out the sports section when it occurred to him that he had not asked Miriam about her day. As he approached the kitchen, Paul took notice of the jazz music playing. As it drifted around him, he considered how lucky a man he was.

Miriam moved about effortlessly in her sleek, well-appointed kitchen. Though it suited her tastes, the room, designed by Paul, reminded her of an operating room or a laboratory with its sterile, shiny surfaces: Carrera marble countertops and white, lacquered cabinets accented by an array of stainless steel knives, pots, and pans as well as appliances. Like a large surgical table, a broad counter sat strategically in the middle, where Miriam had filleted a salmon. Using the knife the way Paul had instructed her, she was cutting paper-thin slices of lemon.

As she worked, Paul quietly slipped up behind her. He put his arms around her waist and gave her a peck on the neck.

Without looking up or letting go of the knife, she reached around below his waist and pinched his rear. He smacked her hard on her behind, which made her turn toward him.

"Why did you do that?" she asked.

"Because," he said, "you didn't look to see if it was me!"

They both giggled and passionately kissed, and then they slowly danced about the kitchen. Jazz filtered from speakers that were built into the ceiling.

When the song ended, Miriam moved to return to her cooking. Paul grabbed her once more for a parting kiss.

After a day of worry, the doctor and his tests were the furthest things from her mind. Equally distracted, Paul had forgotten to ask what she had learned about her exam.

# 2

From her early childhood, Miriam struck those around her as special. She not only conveyed a rare intelligence, but she also emitted an aura of one who was destined for greatness. As if confiding a wondrous secret, she often told her parents that she had lived many centuries ago and her original name was Sela. Looking into her deep, hazel eyes, they almost believed her. All along, they indulged her imagination while answering her endless questions about everything under the sun.

Stan and Bernice Walker accepted that their daughter's exceptional features did not mirror theirs; her finely chiseled nose, perfectly formed lips, and soulful eyes resembled a baby goddess. By the time Miriam reached adulthood, she could have convinced the most ardent skeptic that she had lived in ancient Greece and served as inspiration for the artisans at work on their statues.

She might have become a model or actress if raised by a different sort of parents, but pious churchgoers Stan and Bernice instilled in Miriam their moral and religious convictions while also imparting knowledge. They filled their home with children's books, which Miriam quickly finished. She went on to read everything from classic novels to the ancient philosophers to Darwin. She was a naturally gifted student who far surpassed her peers intellectually; nevertheless, with a vivid imagination and athletic prowess,

Miriam also loved to play and make friends. She excelled in sports and in the sciences, socially and artistically. All the while, her proud parents lavished her with attention and love.

Always encouraged to follow her dreams and strive for success, Miriam considered writing or teaching as a profession. She felt that either would be a noble pursuit. Besides, she knew her parents approved, and Miriam trusted them. She heeded their advice because she realized they had her best interests at heart.

As a reward for her stellar performance and moral character through high school, Stan and Bernice gave Miriam an apple-red Mustang convertible for her high school graduation. It was a token of their love. Miriam loved to ride with the top down, her long, coffee strands of hair blowing in the breeze.

Even with an abundance of good fortune and continued praise for her achievements, Miriam was by no means spoiled. She appreciated everything and was determined to earn her own way in the world. Still, like most young women, she wanted to fall in love, but she would put academics first when she entered Winston College, a small, highly competitive liberal arts institution in Connecticut. To balance her coursework, she joined the track team.

The years seemed to race by with academic and athletic honors. The only thing missing was romance when Miriam entered her senior year at Winston. As hard as she worked, the idea of Mr. Right was always in the back of her mind, but Miriam would be patient. Towards the end of her senior year, Miriam and her roommate Robyn Rogers decided they needed a weekend break to visit Robyn's sister Bridget, a student at Columbia University in New York.

In contrast to Miriam's dark features and statuesque frame, Robyn was diminutive, barely reaching the five-foot mark. Robyn also had blonde hair and blue eyes, as did many of her Minnesota hometown girlfriends, who had Swedish immigrant roots. When she was with Miriam, Robyn couldn't help but notice how they made a striking pair as polar opposites. To say the least, heads turned when they entered a room.

Like Miriam, Robyn was bright and good-natured, but she and Miriam had little else in common. For one thing, Robyn easily dated and seemed to settle when choosing her boyfriends. Characteristically, Robyn had just broken up with yet another steady boyfriend, so for different reasons, she looked forward to a weekend diversion in the Big Apple. Miriam didn't understand why her best friend wasn't more selective with men; she would wait for the one and only Mr. Right.

The two took the train from Hartford to Manhattan, and as it pulled into Grand Central Station, Miriam could almost hear a voice saying, "Okay, Miriam, you're here! Now shake up your life!" Conveying the same message, Bridget was waving her arms eagerly as the girls disembarked. A little chill rippled down the back of Miriam's neck, as if something significant was about to happen.

"We'll drop off your bags, and then I'll show you around Manhattan," Bridget announced with authority. "Great!" the two visitors chimed, both trying to mask a twinge of nervousness.

For transportation, they took a bus. While circling Central Park and riding down Park Avenue, Miriam was glued to the window. Passing renowned museums, exclusive shops, and grand residences, she couldn't decide which impressed her most. Deciding to take a walk on Fifth Avenue, the girls joined the throngs of others on the sidewalks. Adopting a stride as if they, too, had somewhere in particular to go, they tried not to look like tourists.

"Doesn't anyone work in this town?" she asked Bridget. "It's two in the afternoon!"

Bridget smiled and quipped, "We're not working, are we?"

"Guess you're right," Miriam replied. People came to Manhattan for all sorts of reasons. The girls had a full agenda of their own, including to visit Radio City Music Hall and tour the Empire State Building.

By late afternoon, they returned to Bridget's dorm room for a rest. Just as Miriam was wondering what Bridget had in store for the evening, her host said, "By the way, we will each have an escort for tonight. They are frat boys, but don't get the wrong idea. They're good guys. We're meeting them at eight downstairs."

Again, that little chill passed down Miriam's neck to her spine, and she almost wished Bridget hadn't said anything about dates until later. She needed to take a nap!

Surprisingly, however, she closed her eyes, and after what felt like a few minutes, Miriam felt a hand on her back. "Rise and shine," Robyn said, "time to get up and get ready!"

As anxious as Miriam felt, it didn't help that the guys were late. After fifteen minutes, Bridget said, "Don't worry! They really are good guys. They're probably thirty minutes late on purpose, thinking they would be waiting for us, so let's go back up to my room and make it happen!" Sure enough, at eight thirty, the phone peeled off three short rings.

Entering the lobby, Miriam spotted three young men who were obviously waiting for dates. Two had jet black hair, eyes and rather swarthy complexions to match, while the third had red hair and green eyes. Miriam chuckled because he reminded her of Christmas. No Prince Charmings in that bunch, but they were at least nicely outfitted in freshly pressed, buttoned-down-collared shirts and dress slacks. She scanned the area for another potential trio of guys but found none, so she had to assume these were the right ones.

"Hi guys," Bridget sang out, confirming what Miriam had already resigned to be the situation. "Guys, I want you to meet my sister Robyn and her friend Miriam Walker." Without catching her breath, she continued, "They go to school in Hartford. Girls, meet

Jim Dalton and Jerry Seymour. And the redhead here isn't Howdy Doody; he's Arty Robinson." Arty rolled his eyes, so Bridget quickly apologized and said that she was just kidding. Arty didn't find her joke funny, but he shook hands with Miriam and Bridget in a good-natured manner. They all departed, enjoying the cool freshness of the March evening air.

The guys attempted to be the other kind of cool. When they caught a cab, the guys offered their laps to the girls. Bridget and Robyn accepted, but Miriam opted for the front seat. Miriam ignored their jokes about her being a little church girl. There was no Prince Charming back there for her to impress! Even so, she was determined to enjoy the evening.

They had dinner at a restaurant on the corner of 57th Street and Avenue of the Americas. The atmosphere wasn't fancy, but the food was well-prepared. A lively conversation ensued, and all, except Miriam, took part. Through most of the meal, she was many miles away in thought, although a glass of Chablis during diner loosened her up a bit, especially since she rarely drank.

After, the group decided to walk down the Avenue of the Americas to a blues club. It was packed with other young people. Despite the aroma of stale beer and cloud of cigarette smoke that enveloped the room like a London fog, Miriam loved blues and enjoyed the rest of the evening. It wasn't a bad night after all. Tomorrow was Saturday—actually, Saturday was today by the time the girls arrived home—and Miriam noted that it was one of her lucky days. (Monday was the other.) She went to bed with positive thoughts.

After the late night, they didn't get moving until around noon, so they decided to enjoy a leisurely afternoon with lunch at a downtown bistro followed by some museum visits. They would go to a jazz club in the Village that night—without dates. Robyn and Miriam had hoped for a relaxing tour, but Bridget guided her two companions like Sherman marching on Georgia from one museum to the next. After three hours of speeding past exhibits, Robyn took charge. "Let's slow things down," she said, passing a boutique that appealed to her. "Besides, I want something new to wear tonight." Miriam took the opportunity to sit and daydream while her friend tried on a series of outfits.

Later that evening, the three took the subway to Greenwich Village. Miriam, a small-town girl, wasn't thrilled about a nighttime subway ride, but Bridget said she rode it all the time. "I'll protect you!" she promised, making Miriam glad that Bridget was with them. Once in the Village amidst people with hairdos and attire that seemed more like costumes than regular dress, Miriam felt like she was on a movie set. Though over-stimulated by sights, sounds and smells, she picked up the distinct notes of jazz above all the other distractions. As she approached the door to the club, the taunting rhythm tickled her ears and lured her inside. She was in heaven.

Around eleven, the band took a break, and one its members joined the girls at the table. David Lawrence, a friend and on-again-off-again boyfriend of Bridget's, had graduated from Columbia the year before with a PhD in criminal psychology. Average in appearance with his brown hair and eyes, he had a distinct look of intelligence that made David appealing. Though they were not committed, Miriam noted that Bridget and David had something going on because they shared a passionate kiss.

Miriam smiled, wondering what it would be like to have a passionate guy in her life. Fat chance! She was not the sort of gal to enjoy a fling or, for that matter, any causal connection.

Out of frustration, Miriam perused the room. Was she looking for something or someone? She didn't know. As she focused on the front door, she spotted a young man entering with another fellow. Casually dressed in a plaid shirt, jeans, and sneakers, he looked familiar to Miriam, but she knew that she has never met him. As she locked her eyes on the guy, David saw the young man and his companion.

"Paul, Randy—over here!" David's voice resonated across the room. In acknowledgment, the two waved and made their way toward the table. "Everyone meet Paul Rippington and Randy Desmond!" David said with sheer exhilaration.

Miriam had yet to unlock her gaze from the one that David had called Paul. *What's going on?* Miriam wondered.

"Hi," Paul casually said to Miriam. Randy followed with the same greeting.

"Hi," said Miriam, but really only to Paul. Reflexively, she said, "Have a seat." Paul quickly grabbed the empty chair beside her. Both privately felt their pulses rise. Although they had already been introduced, Miriam said, "Hi, Paul, my name is Miriam Walker." She wanted to know everything about him. "Are you a New Yorker?"

"No, I live in Connecticut—Hartford, actually. I'm an attorney. I practice law there. I'm just here for the weekend with Randy. What about you, Miriam?" He liked saying her name.

By now, Miriam realized that all her years of going to church were being rewarded. Her prayers were answered! Prince Charming had taken his place right next to her. Miriam explained to Paul that she, too, lived in Hartford. "I'm a senior at Winston College."

"Is that so?" Paul said. He broadly grinned, realizing that they lived in the same town. "What a small world."

Miriam returned his smile, knowing that "The Lord works in strange and mysterious ways." There were no accidents. Though the break had ended with David and the other musicians returning to the stage, Miriam failed to notice, even though she subconsciously decided that jazz would forever be her favorite music.

Paul had captivated her mind and soul. Would body be next? She expected so. She didn't want the night to end, but Miriam and

Paul said their goodbyes—at four in the morning—with a date planned for Monday night. Monday, Miriam noted, was her other lucky day! She hoped that this Monday would be no exception. As the group broke up, with Miriam and her two girlfriends turning to take the subway back to Columbia, Paul called, "I'll call you at eight tomorrow night, Miriam!"

Sunday was a blur. Miriam returned to school in a cloud of daydreams. Besides thoughts of Paul, nothing else registered. She had met her Prince Charming. When the phone rang at eight on the dot Sunday night, Miriam was ready. They talked for four hours about everything from family and religion to their likes and dislikes, their goals and their dreams. Before their conversation climaxed at midnight, both Miriam and Paul knew that Monday night's date was going to be a special one for them both.

# 3

For their first date, Paul and Miriam had agreed to meet at a restaurant in downtown Hartford. Arriving separately was merely a formality. From the moment that the restaurant hostess escorted them to their table, the only tension between them stemmed from the anticipation of romance.

Requesting a booth so they could sit close, Paul motioned for Miriam to slide in first. He was left-handed and politely wanted to avoid bumping her while eating. She wouldn't have cared. The more contact, the better.

They exchanged more stories about each other's pasts, and when their entrees came, they shared their food as well. Paul, unable to wait to kiss Miriam, impulsively pulled her head towards his. She blissfully obliged. For the first time ever, she felt what most would call "butterflies" and wondered if Paul had a similar sensation.

As if reading her mind, he asked, "Did you feel that?"

"Feel what?" Miriam replied. She was playing coy, but he knew. They continued to kiss, so the waiter discreetly left them alone with the check.

After dinner, they walked to a nearby jazz club. The singer was a middle-aged woman who must have been a knockout in her youth. She purred a soft melody, which enabled Miriam and Paul to converse without raising their voices. Miriam loved that Paul was a great listener. She also found him to be quite interesting. In turn, Paul found Miriam to be fascinating. Oh, and it didn't hurt that she was exceedingly attractive. When they danced, they might as well have been the only two people in the place. Fixated on one another, they knew it was true love.

Following the jazz interlude, they went to a late-night café for dessert. It was a means to extend their night, since neither was hungry. Finding a secluded booth, they kissed until one in the morning, when they decided that they had better end the evening. When Paul took Miriam back to her dorm, it was hard to separate, but they would be seeing one another the next night and the next and the next.

Their relationship continued through the remainder of the school year. When Miriam graduated, her parents and Paul sat together. Officially, they were a couple. Before her graduate program began, Miriam, who was not the kind of gal to vacation with a boyfriend, didn't think twice about taking a two-week trip to the Bahamas with Paul. She wished only that their days of snorkeling, swimming, and love could continue forever.

They didn't move in together, but they made a point of having dinner as a couple almost every night. After separating for the evening, they would manage a good-night call before bed. Compatible in every way, they never exchanged an anxious or awkward moment. Even when silence set in because they had nothing more to say, they were content.

After Miriam completed graduate school, Miriam's parents and Paul once more watched together as Miriam strolled across the stage to receive her degree. If her next step could have been down the wedding aisle, Paul would have been thrilled, but he agreed to wait until Miriam first earned her doctorate in child psychology and then established her practice. While Miriam considered Paul to be her Prince Charming, she was not the type to act like a princess.

She considered starting her own practice, but when she received an offer to join an established children's psychology group in Hartford, she was relieved and happy to accept. About the same time, Paul and a fellow attorney, Leonard Rappaport, decided to leave the large firm that employed them and start their own law practice with two other attorneys. Paul, Leonard, Steve Drummond, and Brian Perkins were destined to be the among the most successful law firms in the area.

With his life going so well for him, Paul sensed only one dark cloud. He missed his parents, who had been killed by a drunk driver when he was a junior in college. The way the situation was handled prompted Paul to take the LSAT and apply to law school. The driver walked freely after being found guilty of manslaughter; through a legal technicality, his attorney had managed to divert this man from going to jail. That had happened ten years ago, and Paul was driven to right the wrong in some small way by being a positive influence in the legal profession.

Paul was a patient man. He had waited two years from the time he first asked Miriam to marry him before she was ready. When they finally set a date, the two agreed that they would both offer sixty percent to the relationship; their marriage would always take priority.

Financially well off, they honeymooned in Bermuda and returned to a five-bedroom home in an exclusive, gated neighborhood in the suburbs. Making the place their own, they chose sleek, contemporary décor that offered coziness and warmth. To select furniture and artwork, they took several buying trips to New York, always allowing time to visit the pub in Greenwich Village where they first met. Eventually, their home was everything they hoped and more—modern, bright, airy and homey. With numerous friends, they anticipated hosting many parties and impromptu get-togethers.

Their first official guests were Miriam's parents. Paul was responsible for preparing the steaks, so the others kept him company by the patio grill. A soft, mid-June breeze circulated the tempting aroma of rib-eyes and charcoal.

"How much longer will it be?" asked Miriam in her usual playful tone. "Dad is drooling."

"The steaks aren't the cause of that," her father said with a laugh. At the same time, he gave his wife a hug and quick kiss on the cheek.

"Dad, cut that out," Miriam said in her lighthearted way. "You and Mom are too old to be acting like teenagers." Though it was funny to see her parents that way, she hoped she and Paul would always be as loving with one another.

More than ever, Stan and Bernice were proud of Miriam. Their daughter had made a life for herself, filled with happiness and accomplishments. Paul was a good husband for her; they supported her choice from the very beginning. The only wish left was to have a grandchild, and they hoped such a blessing would happen soon.

After dinner, they relaxed in the family room. For a housewarming gift, her parents gave Miriam and Paul a photo album. It was a pictorial family history, beginning with Miriam's great-grandparents. Paul looked on, but his thoughts kept drifting to his parents. Though sad that they were not alive to be part of this night, he somehow felt as if that they were there, watching over his shoulder.

As Paul forced his attention back to the conversation, Bernice was telling a story about her grandmother's father, Edward Michael Elmore, who was supposed to have been a magician in Virginia during the Civil War. Family lore also said that he could predict the future. Known to entertain people on many occasions at balls thrown in Richmond, Edward had supposedly foretold of the Emancipation Proclamation, the assassination of Abraham Lincoln, and the historic scandal in President Grant's term. No one, however, predicted Edward's death, which occurred from a blood clot in his brain at Bernice's grandmother's wedding. While greeting guests at the reception, he had simply collapsed to the floor.

Since Edward, no other male children had been born into that family. From the first time Miriam heard that tale, she made up her mind that if she ever had a son, she would name him Edward Michael. She privately considered the sound of Edward Michael Rippington and liked it, all the while wondering what kind of contributions such a son would give to the world.

# 4

To Miriam's surprise, it was nine in the morning, and she was just waking up. The day before, Miriam's doctor had told her she was pregnant. The evening before, she and Paul had enjoyed some amorous time, before and after dinner. Several hours ago, while it was still dark outside, Paul had dressed and left for an early meeting at the courthouse. At that time, she had been feeling queasy, but just told Paul she had a little headache. Miriam didn't have any morning appointments, so he moved about quietly to let her go back to sleep.

She had intended to tell Paul the good news last night, but the time never seemed right. Her plan was to relay the news before bed, but they weren't exactly talking in bed. After, she had fallen asleep exhausted. Since her schedule was open until one o'clock, Miriam picked up the phone to call Paul and ask if he would meet her for an early lunch. If so, she would tell him then.

The phone rang in her hand, which made her jump.

"Hello?" For an inexplicable reason, she felt nervous.

"Mrs. Rippington, this is Jennifer with Dr. Greene's office.

"Yes?" *Why is she calling?* Miriam wondered. "Is there anything wrong?"

"No, no. There's no need to worry, Mrs. Rippington," the nurse replied. "Dr. Greene would like you to come in on Friday for some prenatal screens. It is strictly a routine visit. Would nine o'clock be okay?"

"Just give me a moment to check my schedule," said Miriam. Since it was the week between Christmas and New Year's, many of her clients were vacationing and her schedule was light. Even so, she needed a minute to catch her breath. Miriam realized she would have to calm down, stop worrying. She inhaled and exhaled a few times. "I'll be right there," she finally replied.

After Miriam hung up the phone, she decided not to pop the news over lunch. She'd tell him over a quiet dinner. Besides, she was starving and needed to eat a full breakfast—immediately! While sipping her morning coffee, she noticed that its aroma was exceptionally strong. The day before, she had almost gagged over the distinct smells in the doctor's office: alcohol, ointments, and even fresh paint in the waiting room. So early in her pregnancy, Miriam realized her body had turned into a totally different mechanism.

On her way to the clinic, Miriam considered postponing the baby news until New Year's Eve; it was only a few days away, and she would have undergone her additional medical tests by then. She mentally weighed her options, at last deciding to go ahead with her plans to surprise him that night. Somehow, she managed to conduct her afternoon appointments in her usual professional manner, but as soon as the last patient and his mom left, she couldn't wait to leave the office and almost left her briefcase behind! She was running things through her mind to determine the best way to broach the pregnancy to Paul.

Miriam knew that Paul would be excited, but as happy as she wanted to be, she inexplicably felt that something wasn't quite right with the baby. She had no idea what the problem could be, but her intuition told her that she should be concerned. Driving home, Miriam made up her mind to tell Paul about the pregnancy, but she would keep her worries to herself.

Although she'd slept late and handled a light patient load, Miriam was too tired to prepare an elaborate meal when she got home. Instead, she called Chez Pierre, the couple's favorite local French restaurant, and made a reservation. She would tell him over dessert. She hoped Paul would find it to be his best dessert ever. In the meantime, she would take a nice long warm bubble bath to rest and calm her nerves.

An hour later, Paul entered the bedroom, where he found Miriam sitting wrapped in a bathrobe in front of her make-up mirror. She turned to smile at Paul, trying not to look anxious or smile like she knew something that he didn't. Letting him know about the reservation, Miriam added that he had an hour before they needed to leave for dinner. He approached her, as if to begin a romantic interlude, but Miriam suggested that he shower and shave instead. "No need to rush things tonight," she said with a wink.

At Chez Pierre, Miriam and Paul were greeted warmly by the maître d' and shown to their favorite table. They enjoyed the French menu, but what Miriam and Paul most loved about the place was its signature jazz trio. The female singer, backed by two male musicians, had a broad vocal range, from gently purring slow ballads to belting out the songs that reminded them of Ella Fitzgerald.

As Paul scanned the wine list, Miriam innocently said that she really didn't care for any. "What's the matter, honey?" Paul was suspicious. "You always like a glass of wine with dinner."

"Maybe I'll have a glass later, but not now," she said. Later for her was going to be eight months. After the main course, she ordered chocolate mousse, and Paul chose cherries jubilee for dessert. Still, Miriam hadn't told him. As the waiter moved away from the table, Miriam felt a lump building in her throat. The time was now or never.

"Paul, you know that I went to see Dr. Greene. You had remarked that I might be pregnant. Well, I am!"

"You're pregnant?" he asked, as if his ears were playing a trick on him.

"Yes, sweetheart, I am!"

With that, Paul leaned over to share one of their remarkably passionate kisses. In a way, the kiss reflected the awesome miracle that they had performed. This baby would be the product of their love for each other. Miriam would keep her worries to herself, for now. There would be enough time to worry later.

After finishing the evening romantically in bed, they both woke up early to continue where they had left off the night before. With New Year's approaching, their work schedules were light. They later talked about how they would celebrate the end of the holiday season and the beginning of a promising new year. There would be no champagne for Miriam, and a boisterous affair did not appeal to either of them. Other than Paul's law firm party on the thirtieth, they did not have any other obligations. Some friends were having big parties, so Miriam and Paul didn't feel like they had to show. New Year's Eve would be theirs to ring in alone. Next year, they would have a little chaperone.

# 5

Returning to work on the second of January, Paul felt his emotions running in all directions. The idea of becoming a father consumed his thoughts. How would a baby affect his relationship with Miriam? How would he handle his new responsibilities? Paul decided that he would manage his personal life like his law practice. He would balance his time and order the priority of each situation. The idea was a good one, if only in theory. With no clue as to what the future would hold, he was about to learn what life as a father was all about.

His experiences growing up made Paul Rippington self-motivated. As a young boy, he saw his father go to work early and come home late. James Rippington, Paul's father, was a self-made millionaire. Joseph, James's father, had come to America at the beginning of the twentieth century with his mother, Regina, and his brother, Richard. The three had left England as well as a family scandal. Joseph's father was rumored to be John Rippington, who was suspected of being Jack the Ripper. Jack the Ripper had terrorized London in 1888 by brutally victimizing prostitutes in the Whitechapel district, an impoverished neighborhood filled with pubs and prostitutes. Joseph Rippington had told his son James that the rumor was true; supposedly, he had seen the evidence as a young boy. To escape the horror and disgrace, Paul's great grand-mother had taken her two young sons to America.

When Regina and sons Joseph and Richard arrived in Boston in 1901, they moved in with her sister Frances in the Cambridge area. Young Joseph was a model student there, while his younger brother Richard was quite the opposite. Richard hated school and was rather rebellious. He was constantly skipping classes to spend time with his hoodlum friends. Joseph tried to get Richard to give up that sort of life, but Richard wouldn't listen. The following year, Richard ran away, never to be heard from again—or so the family thought.

Regina was heartbroken and fearful of what Richard would become. At the same time, she was relieved to devote her life to ensuring Joseph's education. In fact, Joseph graduated from high school with honors and attended Harvard on a full scholarship. Graduating at the top of his class, summa cum laude, he moved to New York, where he got a job as a law clerk on Wall Street. A bright and talented attorney, Joseph became a partner in his firm and married Harriet Brooks, one of the most sought-after Boston socialites, within three years. On the fast track, barely one year after their wedding, he and Harriet had their first child, Samantha.

Both Joseph and Harriet were proud of Samantha. Going against convention, they wanted their daughter to graduate col-lege and apply her talented mind to a meaningful area of work. Although Samantha did well in school and hoped to pursue medi-cine, the universities were not keen on offering spots to women for medical studies. Samantha graduated from Bryn Mawr College and, with her father's financial backing, opened a medical clinic for low-income families. She hired young physicians just starting out to staff it, and while many moved on to more profitable practices, a few loyal doctors remained with the clinic.

To earn additional income that would support the clinic,

Samantha and her partner, Susan Murphy, designed a doctor's bag made of Italian leather, which they began advertising in medical publications. Immediately, they began receiving orders from physicians across the country. Production began with a half-dozen employees, but the women had ideas for expansion. Within one year, the women had a full-blown factory and warehouse. After ten years, they sold the business to a group of investors, and the money afforded them the luxury of devoting their lives too philanthropic work. Samantha founded the Rippington Foundation to help the poor.

In her later years, Samantha once told a reporter that she had been guided by what she believed to be a divine force. She even referred to the power as Uriel, whom she described like an angel or familiar. The reporter thought she might have been suffering with dementia, so he cut the reference of Uriel from the printed story. Only Samantha had the original manuscript with mention of her guide. Undaunted, Samantha often spoke of Uriel as influential to her success.

While she had accomplished extraordinary deeds for a woman of her time, Samantha regretted only that she had never married or had a child. Only those who were closest to her knew that not marrying was her choice. Fearful that her grandfather, John Rippington, might have passed along a demonic gene, she refused to take the chance of bearing a child of that nature.

While they had been the ones to pass along the story of her grandfather, Samantha's mother and father did not believe in a "bad seed." Consequently, when she was nine years old, Samantha became a big sister with the birth of James.

James demonstrated a fascination with biology when he was a young boy. Curious, he dissected frogs until becoming quite adept with a scalpel. Secretly, Joseph worried about his son, but he didn't have the heart to tell Harriet. Instead, Joseph tried to divert

James's fascination for cutting open living creatures to analyzing businesses.

After James graduated, he went to work as a runner on Wall Street, deciding that he would spend his life making money to make his father proud. For five years, his job was to comb businesses in Manhattan, looking for investors in the stock market. During that time, he made numerous, valuable connections, who included some of the most influential men in New York. As James moved up the ladder, he maintained his contacts and eventually formed an investment firm with two others. They were called Reynolds, Goldberg, and Rippington.

At the age of twenty-five, James married Grace Henderson, who reminded him of his mother in her beauty. The following year, Grace gave birth to Paul.

Paul grew up in an affluent home. The family mansion in Cambridge was among the finest. They belonged to the most exclusive clubs and often traveled to Europe. Paul had everything he desired, but he was expected to make his own way as an adult. His parents' auto accident and untimely death determined that his precise path to success would be law. As fate would have it, Paul was already a promising young attorney when he met Miriam Walker.

Paul did not know that his father's Uncle Richard, the "bad seed" who had once run away, had been partly responsible for his parents' accident. Uncle Richard had tampered with the brakes of James's car in a twisted plot of revenge for Joseph's successful life. No one suspected Richard because he rarely had anything to do with anyone in the family, other than occasionally asking for money. He also covered his tracks.

As his life passed before his eyes upon his death, however, Uncle Richard would pay for his crime.

# 6

September thirteenth started out to be a breezy day, and a tall holly brushed the bedroom window screen. Miriam woke with a start.

"Paul, wake up," Miriam said, nudging Paul. "It's time."

Paul rolled over. "Are you sure, honey?"

"Of course, I am."

As she dressed, Miriam wondered whether the thirteenth would prove to be lucky, if not long. Her labor slowly progressed, and she gave birth to Edward Michael Rippington at one minute before eleven o'clock that night. He was a beautiful baby with a full head of thick, dark-brown hair and matching dark-brown eyes. At six pounds, four ounces, and nineteen inches long, Edward was suddenly more special to Miriam and Paul than they ever could have imagined. Having a son to carry on the Rippington name was an added blessing. However, a few hours later, they noticed that something was wrong with their baby.

Little Edward's head began to swell, so slowly at first that it was almost unnoticeable. Soon, however, the change was evident. They frantically buzzed for help, and as soon as the nurse spotted the baby, she called Dr. Westin. An examination confirmed that their son had hydrocephalus, which was an abnormal accumulation of cerebrospinal fluid in the brain. The medical condition not only caused the head to look large, but it increased pressure inside the skull. Miriam and Paul were terribly shaken as they learned about the potential for convulsions, mental disability, and even death. The doctor immediately ordered tests. Also, because of the swelling, the fluid had to be drained as quickly as possible. Edward would be fitted with a shunt immediately.

Signing the consent papers that allowed the shunt operation to take place, Miriam and Paul would have given their lives to make their little boy well. During the hour they waited for the procedure to take place, Miriam mostly prayed while Paul paced. Finally, Dr. Westin met with Paul and Miriam. He told them that before they began, they noticed that the swelling had stopped on its own.

"The only thing that we can do now is to wait to see if the fluid might drain on its own," said Dr. Westin. "I wish I could be more optimistic, but the possibility of severe brain damage is extremely high."

Dr. Westin went on to say that Paul and Miriam should prepare for the inevitable: that their son would not live a normal life. If he survived more than a few months, Edward would require around-the-clock care. They would probably need to institutionalize him. Furious and upset that anyone would suggest that her son's needs would be too much for her to handle, Miriam asked Dr. Westin to leave her room.

Miriam had made up her mind. She would take her baby home and raise him to be a functioning child. Paul agreed. Edward was their flesh and blood, though he had to stay in the hospital for an extended period. In addition to administering additional tests and stabilizing his condition, the staff had to make certain Paul and Miriam would be able to handle any complications that could arise. Paul and Miriam believed that their love would overcome any obstacles.

After Miriam was released from the hospital, she returned daily to be with little Edward. He was placed in the infants' ICU unit with the premature babies. There, Miriam stayed with him, monitoring his condition from hour to hour. Noting the swelling of his skull, she was worried, and with plenty of reason.

Brain damage was their primary fear. Infants with brain swelling had survived before shunts were used, but most died quickly. Of those who lived past infancy, the majority were severely brain damaged. Only a tiny percentage lived normal lives, so even though Edward's swelling had subsided, damage could have already occurred. Though Paul was not typically one to pray, he joined Miriam in praying for a miracle.

A miracle, indeed, unfolded before their eyes. At ten days old, Edward was beginning to respond to his surroundings. Weeks before what was normal for healthy babies, he smiled at his parents, as if to acknowledge their love. The word of his progress traveled throughout the hospital, and nurses and doctors from all areas dropped by to see him.

After the first week, Paul returned to work. To ease Miriam's burden, he hired a full-time nanny. Highly efficient, she immediately began helping Miriam prepare the nursery, which was ready when the hospital unexpectedly released Edward early at the end of the second week.

During the drive home from the hospital, Edward unexpectedly started to cry. Miriam tried to console him with a pacifier and her gentle touch, but he continued. As they approached a busy intersection, Edward cried unlike he ever had before. It was to such a point that Paul pulled the car over. Right at that time, another car ran a red light through the intersection. If Paul had not stopped, they would have been hit head-on by the reckless driver.

Turning their attention back to Edward, they realized that he had not only stopped crying, but was cooing. How odd! What a fortunate coincidence—or was it? Either way, Paul and Miriam considered their son to be a blessing.

"Paul, I wouldn't say this to anyone else—they would think I am crazy—but I believe Edward is special. Do you know what I'm saying?"

"Yes, Miriam, I do. I have to agree."

Edward did not so much as whimper the rest of the drive home. When they removed him from the car, he gazed at the sky, the trees, the grass, and the house as if he were taking in the world around him. When a bird chirped happily, Edward turned his head toward the sound and smiled. Paul and Miriam looked at each other with disbelief. Were they imagining their son's capabilities? No. Their child was special; of that they were certain.

Once in his nursery, they again watched in amazement as Edward looked around the room. His eyes traveled from the ceiling painted with clouds to a barnyard of stuffed animals, and Edward began to coo at his new surroundings. Paul and Miriam could hardly wait to find out what else Edward was going to do to amaze them.

א

His first two weeks at home passed so easily and enjoyably that Miriam could not believe it was already time for Edward's one-month checkup. To the pediatric specialist's utter shock, Edward's brain had been reduced in size to one-quarter the amount of a normal one-month-old brain, and the hydrocephalus had compartmentalized to an area within his brain. The physician had never seen nor read anything like it.

"By all accounts, Edward should have been dead by now," the doctor said in all honesty. "His progress is utterly amazing. Brain damage, however, remains an imminent concern. He's too young to gauge what his limitations will be, but the coming months will be critical. We'll just have to monitor Edward closely and address his special needs as they arise."

Miriam, however, was not concerned about Edward's mental aptitude. She didn't dare tell the doctor what she and Paul had witnessed. He would want to institutionalize her! Still, with a diminished brain capacity, her son might have physical problems. She would not focus on that. Instead, when Paul came home for dinner that night, Miriam gave him the good news about the hydrocephalus while diminishing the bad news about Edward's brain size.

Paul, who was more cautious, knew that it could be years before the extent of Edward's problems came to light. Miriam, however, reminded Paul that Edward was a gift and a miracle. They would deal with any issues that arose matter-of-factly.

# 7

A few days after Edward's medical checkup, he became fussy after eating. Miriam had been unable to nurse him, so she was feeding him formula, which was causing the baby digestive distress. When Miriam called the pediatrician's office, the nurse made time in the doctor's schedule to see Edward that day.

Less alarmed than his nurse or Miriam, Dr. Westin examined Edward and then told Miriam to give him goat's milk.

"Really?" she asked. "Isn't that an old-fashioned remedy?"

"It might be old-fashioned, but it's as effective as anything you can buy on the market today," Dr. Westin said.

To Miriam's surprise, Edward adjusted well to the goat's milk. She, nevertheless, had to get used to the new, unpleasant odor of his burps!

Overall, however, making accommodations for her baby was her pleasure. In certain ways, Edward made life easier. When Bernice arrived to visit her grandchild and daughter, for instance, Miriam opened the front door before her mother rang the bell.

"How did you know that I was at the door?" asked a puzzled Bernice.

"Mom, you won't believe this, but Edward started whimpering," said Miriam. "I've noticed that he makes the same kind of fuss each time someone comes to the house. This time, I went downstairs, and here you are at the door!"

"Are you sure?" asked Bernice.

"I am now!" Miriam said with utter certainty.

"Well, he is named for my great-grandfather, who was known to have psychic abilities!" said Bernice. The mother and daughter talked about Edward's namesake, the famous prognosticator of Civil War days. Neither woman, however, mentioned how the original Edward collapsed and died immediately at the family wedding, but Miriam shuddered at the thought.

From time to time, a sense of dread hovered at the back of Miriam's mind, but she shook it off. She and Paul spoke only of Edward's steady growth and remarkable awareness. He developed chubby arms and legs, and his skin was a healthy pink, even though his head remained ever so slightly enlarged.

At times, he seemed to be drawn into his own little world. On other occasions, he demonstrated an uncanny perceptiveness, as when he seemed to know when a visitor had arrived or when Paul was just home from the office. She prayed that his special abilities would compensate for any problems that might arise from the hydrocephalus. Edward, for instance, could not lift his head like most babies at three months of age, but he was clearly more attuned to his environment. Miriam constantly read books to Edward, and his eyes followed the pages like a child of five years or older. Extraordinarily, too, Edward was four months old when he said his first words.

"Hey there," Edward had said. Paul and Miriam clearly heard him.

Rather than report his advancements to Dr. Westin, Miriam decided she would let Edward speak for himself. On his six-month checkup, the baby took that opportunity. "Hello," he said plainly to Dr. Westin. Flabbergasted, Dr. Westin wanted to run a battery of IQ tests. Miriam, however, refused. She did not want her son to be treated like a lab rat. She also didn't want Edward to become a spectacle for curious minds. "Dr. Westin, let's just acknowledge that Edward, like every child, is special in his own way and leave it at that."

Reluctantly, Dr. Westin agreed to abide by her wishes. Edward would not be another case study for the medical journals. Miriam's assertiveness on the matter was understood by Dr. Westin. He reluctantly decided to drop the matter.

After that episode, Miriam was glad to get Edward home. Thankfully, Paul did not have to work late. At six o'clock, he came through the back door. "How are you, honey bunny?" Paul said.

"I am fine." Miriam's voice sounded tired. "I took Edward to the doctor today for his six-month checkup. Edward said 'hello' to Dr. Westin, who got all excited and wanted to submit our baby to a battery of IQ tests. I wouldn't allow it. I want us to embrace his special gifts, not turn Edward into a freak show."

"That won't happen," said Paul. "We're his parents." Kissing Miriam on the back of her neck, he whispered, "Don't worry."

"Okay," Miriam said. She turned to hug Paul. "Why don't you go up and see him."

"How is the little honey bunny?" Paul asked. He could have held her in his arms for days, but Miriam shifted her stance; she wanted to finish making dinner.

"He's upstairs with the nanny," she said. "He got some routine vaccines today, so he might be sleeping. Go see."

Paul could take a hint. He went up to Edward's nursery, where he found the nanny in the chair, gently rocking Edward while he slept. Paul couldn't help but smile at the sight of his son resting so peacefully. Smiling at the nanny, he whispered a soft hello to her. Paul continued to stand there for a few minutes just to observe his son asleep.

Hearing about Dr. Westin's desire to put Edward under a microscope, he realized that his son's future would not be simple. It seemed crazy that such a little being could cause such a stir. Would his boy grow up to be physically healthy and socially accepted? That was his prayer for Edward.

The nanny placed Edward in his crib, and Paul went downstairs to visit with Miriam while she made the final preparations for dinner. As he reentered the kitchen, Paul heard jazz music. It reminded him of the romantic night they had shared just before he learned that Miriam was pregnant. So much had happened since then. He spontaneously pecked her on the cheek.

"Why did you do that?" Miriam asked. Her tone was one of disbelief.

"What do you mean, honey bunny?" Paul was confused.

"Do you know what you just did?" Miriam asked.

"Sure do!" Paul said. "I kissed you on the cheek."

"Exactly! So, where's the passion?" She expected him to kiss her like he meant it, and Paul readily obliged. "That was much better." After, they broke into a dance around the kitchen. Knowing the nanny was upstairs with Edward gave them the benefit of alone time.

Edward was still sleeping soundly when Paul and Miriam looked in on him after dinner. The nanny's babysitting duties were over for the evening, so Paul and Miriam embraced while they stood over Edward in his crib. Despite all the uncertainties, they welcomed every challenge and opportunity their unique child presented. They were going to do all they could to give him the advantages he deserved to be productive and happy. Devoted to one another, Paul and Miriam were equally dedicated to their son.

Dr. Westin had not given them much hope for Edward to live as a normal adult. Putting aside the baby's exceptional capacity to communicate, the pediatrician still questioned the extent of

Edward's aptitude. Then, putting his mental ability aside, the doctor continued to express concern that Edward would have physical disabilities.

When Edward began to drag himself along the floor using his elbows at nine months, Dr. Westin warned Paul and Miriam not to expect Edward to walk for years. For every grim prognosis, however, Edward presented something positive. At his early age, he had a vocabulary that included *lamp, chair,* and *sofa,* in addition to *Daddy* and *Mama.* Incredibly, nine-month-old Edward could vocalize over one hundred words. Friends, relatives, and bystanders were speechless when they heard such a young little fellow speak so clearly.

Visitors of the Rippingtons also watched with amazement as Edward determinedly navigated from one area to another. He could not pull himself up, but Edward smiled with understanding as Miriam encouraged each facet of his progress.

Edward's extrasensory perceptiveness was also blossoming. Now that he could speak, he constantly notified his parents when a visitor was about to show up or a phone call was eminent. Sometimes, though, Edward detected the presence of those who were not regular people.

One afternoon, Miriam felt that someone was in the car with her as she drove up the driveway. Uncomfortable, she peeked in the rearview mirror. No one was there, but the sense that there was made her shiver. Unable to shake the feeling, she headed inside. The nanny was in the laundry room, so Miriam ran upstairs to check on Edward, who was alone in his crib in the nursery. She stopped at the doorway and peeked inside. Edward was looking ahead and talking. "Uri," she heard him say.

*Uri?* Puzzling over the name, if that's what "Uri" was, Miriam recalled a story Paul had told her about his Aunt Samantha. The eccentric lady claimed to have had a spirit guide named Uriel. The notion that Edward was communicating with a great aunt's spirit guide seemed crazy yet strangely probable.

Miriam couldn't wait for Paul to arrive home that night. The second he walked through the door, she asked him to recount the story. Paul told her that, indeed, his Aunt Samantha had adamantly told him and anyone else who listened that she had received what she called "divine guidance" from her spirit guide whose name was Uriel. Had Edward been talking to this same spirit guide? Miriam shivered, but Paul seemed to shrug it off.

"Doesn't this bother you?" she asked her husband.

"Why should it, Miriam?" he responded. "Either Edward has a terrific imagination or an amazing spiritual guide."

Miriam wasn't so sure. Extra sensory perception was one thing, but she did not like the notion of unidentified beings in her baby's presence. What if Uri or Uriel was a demon spirit?

Refusing to leave Edward alone with the nanny, Miriam noticed that Edward seemed to spend hours watching and listening to *someone* or *something*, but *no one* was there. Determined to get to the bottom of the situation, Miriam tried to speak to Uriel herself. "Uriel, I'm Edward's mother," she would say. "And as his mother, I want to know who you are and why you are here. If you're here to look out for my son's wellbeing, please just say so. If you're a demon, you had better scram before I call in Reverend Michaels and the deacons!"

To distract Edward, Miriam read him book after book and talked to him about everything good under the sun. Edward loved to sit in Miriam's lap while she rocked, talked, and read. He preferred stories were about children who were also special. Though it was a tale for older children, not babies or toddlers, *Charlie and the Chocolate Factory* by Roald Dahl was his favorite.

While visiting the library one day, Miriam decided to do a little research on Roald Dahl. When she started reading about him, she found that Edward and the renowned author coincidentally shared the same birthday: September thirteenth. More surprisingly, though, was that Mr. Dahl was involved in the research and development of brain shunts. He had two children who experienced problems stemming from brain injuries.

Deciding that her inspired research was not simply coincidence, Miriam made up her mind to contact the author. She called his publisher's office. An assistant said she would pass along the message. For no reason other than her gut telling her so, Miriam suddenly felt that Edward and Uriel and Roald Dahl were all connected.

Not sure what Paul would think of her, Miriam shared her thoughts with him. He didn't look at her as if she were crazy. Instead, Paul prompted Miriam to visit a local store that was known for its comprehensive selection of New Age books and publications. Miriam was astounded to find a birthday book which indicated that the guardian angel or spirit guide for the thirteenth day was Uriel. "This is getting out of hand!" she said aloud.

Later that evening, Miriam asked Paul if he knew when Aunt Samantha was born.

"It's recorded in that old family Bible," he said. Paul pulled the book from the shelf. "You're not going to believe this, honey bunny, but Aunt Samantha was born on September thirteenth."

For two solid minutes, complete silence descended. Miriam was stunned. Paul was too busy looking through the Bible to notice. When she had gathered her composure, Miriam told Paul to sit next to her on the sofa and revealed what she had discovered in the birthday book, which she had purchased. She went upstairs and returned with the book. Turning to the page for September thirteenth, she pointed to the appropriate text. "The spirit guide is Uriel," she said. "Edward's been saying 'Uri.'"

They darted upstairs to look in on Edward. He was sleeping quietly. Something extraordinary was happening, but neither one of them knew what all of this meant.

As the weeks went by, Miriam wondered if she would ever hear from Roald Dahl. Fortunately, Edward continued to grow stronger. Highly attuned to his surroundings, he was beginning to lift his head and look from side to side. Both Paul and Miriam were encouraged; it was too early to tell what his range of movement would be. Paul and Miriam hoped and prayed that he would gain full strength and live a full life. Miriam was saying one of her countless silent prayers when the telephone rang, and, somehow, she knew that the caller was Roald Dahl.

"Mrs. Rippington, this is Roald Dahl." The two exchanged pleasant hellos. "I just received word that you have been trying to contact me regarding your son's situation," he continued. "As a parent, I understand what you are going through. How can I be of help to you?"

Though she had contacted him, Miriam could not believe Roald Dahl was telling her that he would like to help Edward. Dahl was explaining that he had founded a trust fund to help children with brain problems. Adding that he would soon be in Hartford for a seminar, Dahl offered to meet with Miriam and her family. Before hanging up, Miriam gathered her nerve to ask if he had ever heard of Uriel.

"So, you're aware of Uriel?" asked Dahl. He went on to say that, yes, Uriel was his lifelong spirit guide. "Your son Edward and I are connected through him."

That was all Miriam needed to hear. She thanked him profusely and expressed that she was looking forward to the meeting. In turn, Dahl told her not to worry. He would do whatever he could to help Edward.

After hanging up the phone, Miriam called Paul. Maybe there was hope for Edward after all. For the first time since Edward's birth, the two were not only optimistic, but they felt that their son had a meaningful future in store.

During the next few weeks, Miriam and Paul talked about the possibilities, and Edward seem to know that something was about to happen. He repeatedly said, "Uri," nodding in conversation, as the meeting date with Roald Dahl approached.

The Rippingtons arranged to meet Roald Dahl at a hotel convention center where the author was speaking. Upon entering the grand lobby, they spotted a tall, distinctive gentleman across the way. When the four met in the middle, the lights flickered. Had they generated a rush of electricity, overloading the circuits?

"Hello! You must be Paul and Miriam Rippington, and this must be little Edward."

Dahl led the Rippingtons to a suite he was using as an office, and there they discussed the options for Edward. Dahl recommended a Boston specialist, Dr. Frank Weller, who researched and treated patients suffering with motor and mental difficulties that result from hydrocephalus at birth. At the same time, Dahl and Edward seemed to have bonded before meeting in person, and Edward exhibited utter contentment in the hours his parents and this important man talked.

A few weeks later, Dr. Weller examined Edward in his Boston office. The physician proclaimed that the child's condition had not only stabilized, but, after reviewing Edward's medical records, Dr. Weller was astounded by the little one's progress. When he learned that they had not given Edward therapy other than their own nurturing, the doctor recommended that the parents continue. "Whatever you're doing for your son is far better than any therapy I could offer," he pronounced.

Paul and Miriam simply treated Edward like they would if he had been what medical science considered normal. They read to him. They took him to the zoo and museums. They enjoyed an array of outdoor outings together, like picnics, bike rides, and boating.

Edward had a custom-made toddler seat that supported his skeleton, enabling him to sit upright and see the world around him.

Although Edward had learned to speak words well before schedule, he his overall verbal skills had not progressed. He communicated using short phrases rather than complete sentences, but his parents and nanny understood him. In turn, Edward fully comprehended what the adults conveyed to him.

Building his motor skills, Edward crawled more efficiently. Using a stuffed, black dog that he called "Blackie" for incentive, his parents made a game of encouraging Edward to crawl here and there to reach his fluffy friend.

For his third birthday, neighborhood kids and his grandparents came for a party to celebrate. A nine-year-old neighbor named Catherine loved being with Edward, and she helped support him so that he could blow out the candles on the cake. When he couldn't blow them out, a five-year-old boy offered his help, yet pretended Edward did the job.

"The children really seemed to take to him," said Stan after the festivities ended and Edward was asleep. Bernice was also beaming because her grandchild was three years old. He was developing, and even though he wasn't *normal*—or perhaps because he was special—he also had friends.

Uri, however, was Edward's closest pal. Whatever Edward said or heard from his spirit guide, Miriam and Paul had come to trust it would benefit the wellbeing of their boy. How else could they assess this relationship, or whatever one should call it? Dr. Weller, for one, had used the word "miracle" to describe Edward's very existence. In fact, the child became an inspiration to the specialist's entire staff.

Indeed, just after Edward's third birthday, he began to walk. He also began communicating in full sentences. Though he was not a big talker, he made his words count rather than babble in the way that most children his age would go on. Edward, for instance, once said to Miriam, "I will someday travel in space, but you shouldn't worry. I'll be safe."

When Miriam shared Edward's statement with Dr. Weller, the physician said, "He's clearly articulate and imaginative." He also cautioned that Edward's differences could hinder his ability to follow a normal path in life. "He's showing signs of autism," Dr. Weller said gently. "On one hand, we can see that he's bright, but Edward's constant involvement with his imaginary friend is disconcerting."

When Miriam later shared Dr. Weller's warning with Paul, the two had to wonder what was precisely going on in Edward's mind. The two went to check on their son, and seemingly understanding his parents' concern, the child said, "Don't worry. Uri will always be here for me."

# 8

From Dr. Weller's caution to Edward's calm, Miriam and Paul wanted to be sure they made healthy decisions on behalf of their son. Dr. Weller suggested that they watch his further growth for two more years. Miriam prayed that when Edward turned five, he would be able to go to kindergarten. They had always protected him, but it might be wise to foster interaction with other children. Paul agreed, and so did Edward!

Just before his fourth birthday, Paul and Miriam decided that they should let Edward attend a prekindergarten program. After mulling over the idea, Miriam and Paul found a small, private school that believed in integrating children with special needs in the general classroom. While Paul was all for the idea, Miriam prayed that Edward would adjust.

Upon arriving on his first day, Edward spotted a schoolyard full of kids playing on swings, slides, and a gigantic jungle gym. He couldn't wait to join them, but he wanted Blackie to come along. "Sweetie, let me keep him with me," said Miriam. "You don't want him to get lost or hurt by accident." Reluctantly, Edward agreed that Blackie should stay with his mom. "It also might be better to go to school without Uri," she added. Miriam did not think the other kids would take to Edward if he started chatting with an unseen spirit.

In response, Edward asked Uri what he thought, and Uri agreed with his mother. "Okay," Edward responded.

Miriam and Edward met Mrs. Norton, the headmistress, in her office. The respected educator had kind brown eyes and a pleasing smile, and she made Edward feel right at home. He was not in the least upset when Miriam left him alone, but his mom didn't do a good job of hiding her tears. "Don't worry," he told her. "I'll be fine!"

After describing the school and explaining the basic rules to Edward, Mrs. Norton took the boy to meet his teacher and classmates. Edward quickly attached himself to Mrs. Mathews, an attractive, blue-eyed blonde with wisdom and intuition that well exceeded her twenty-eight years. She, in turn, loved Edward from the start and made every effort to ensure that he was welcomed by the other children and at ease. Primarily, she encouraged Edward to be himself.

He did not say so, but Edward was a bit overwhelmed. He also didn't reveal that Uri had promised to stay nearby but that Edward should not call upon the spirit guide unless he absolutely needed help.

By this time, Edward had been officially diagnosed with Asperger's Syndrome, a high-functioning form of autism. Defining hallmarks were clumsiness and difficulty expressing emotions. On occasion, Edward would trip over his own feet. When that happened, most of the kids would laugh, which made Edward turn to Uriel for comfort. "Edward," Uri would say, "you must remember that the children are providing a great learning experience. They are teaching you to focus on what you have to do." Uriel's words prevented Edward from withdrawing from the other children, and the idea of making a real friend his own age soon appealed to him. It was to everyone's delight when Edward and William, another four-year-old who preferred to be called Billy, bonded from the start. Throughout the school year, the two boys were inseparable, and their friendship continued over the summer. Generally, however, they played at Edward's home, where he felt most comfortable.

When Edward turned five and entered kindergarten, he began to feel overwhelmed with school. Despite his parents and Uriel's coaxing, he decided to stay home for a few months. While at home, Edward watched television and spent some time with his coloring books and crayons. After three months, Uri convinced Edward to return to school.

He liked other children and looked forward to having them visit him at his house, but the idea of spending time at their homes was disconcerting to Edward. Just the thought of separating from Miriam made him cling to her. With Uriel's urging, however, Edward made the effort to venture out and soon learned to be more comfortable without his mother.

For his first-grade year, Edward was fortunate again to have a kindhearted, perceptive teacher. Ms. Phelps worked closely with Edward to help him channel his natural intelligence towards his subjects. Edward easily understood the concepts, but he struggled to follow instructions that seemed pointless to him. Usually, he grew bored and his mind wandered. For instance, while the other children were learning to count to one hundred, Edward went to stare out the window.

"Edward," Ms. Phelps said, "you must remember that you have to be seated while in we are in class." Distracted from his daydream, he returned to his desk. Edward had already counted thousands of stars, but he obediently attempted to sit still.

After six weeks in the first grade, Edward befriended a girl named Margaret. Margaret was a cute blond with a radiant smile. She and Edward started spending time together over the weekends. Margaret would come over to Edward's house on Saturdays. It didn't matter if it was raining, snowing, or sunny. The two could play for hours without a break—whether out in the backyard or tucked away in Edward's bedroom.

Margaret and Edward grew exceptionally close. It was not unusual for them to kiss and snuggle together. There was a wooded area behind Edward's house where they would go to talk and kiss. Edward really liked kissing Margaret, and she liked kissing him. This went on for a few months.

One Saturday afternoon in December, while Margaret was at Edward's house, she asked Edward to dance with her. Edward felt uncomfortable with the idea of dancing because the nanny was there. "I don't want to," he said. Margaret got offended and called her mother to come get her. This was the end of their courtship.

# 9

Edward would celebrate his seventh birthday at a local carnival with Catherine and Billy. He couldn't wait to ride a Shetland pony, so Paul and Miriam gave him a cowboy hat and boots for his gift, along with a cap gun and holster. After enjoying rides on the pony and carousel, cotton candy and games, they returned to the Rippington's home for ice cream and cake.

When he blew out the candles on his cake, decorated with cowboys and horses, Edward announced that his wish was to be like the other kids.

"You are like other children," Miriam softly said to him. "The difference is that you have been given special gifts unlike anyone else. Billy and Catherine, too, have their own gifts as well."

Billy asked, "What special gifts do I have?"

Miriam smiled. "I think you know, so why don't you tell us?"

Billy grinned and said, "I'm the best goalie on my soccer team!"

Catherine smiled. Her gift was her sensitivity and concern for others, but she didn't want to sound boastful by admitting it.

Edward, meanwhile, continued to put his abilities to important use, and Miriam learned to listen when he cautioned her about her driving. Several times, his forewarning prevented accidents, and that never failed to astound Miriam, and Edward always accepted her praise with modesty.

Neither Paul nor Miriam could predict what Edward would do or whom he might save in the future, or what role Uriel would play in the end.

# 10

When Halloween arrived, Edward chose to be Superman, a character that made him feel big, strong—invincible. Growling like the figure he had read about in hundreds of comic books, the bulky boy went outside to see how the neighbor's St. Bernard, named Midas, would react. In response, Midas cocked his head, which made Edward laugh. Edward started chasing Midas around the yard until dog and boy wore each other out with their game. Edward dropped to the ground, and Midas began licking his friend's flushed face.

"You know I was just playing, didn't you?" Edward said. Of course, Midas knew that. Of all the human children he had encountered, Midas sensed a different kind of connection with Edward.

His relationship with animals would be among Edward's gifts, all of which he would apply to helping others. The stories about his mindreading Civil War ancestor were fascinating, but Edward did not want applause or wealth for his talents. He simply wanted to do good deeds and make others happy.

His inability to connect with other children who didn't understand him was the only discontent in Edward's life. Since he often withdrew into his own world and rarely made eye contact, boys and girls his age called him "zombie" and other names, but never to his face. Even so, Edward knew. He knew that the kids didn't quite know what to make of him. They marveled at his intelligence but were puzzled by his awkwardness and clumsiness.

After a particularly tough day at school, Uriel brightened Edward's mood by promising to introduce the boy to his colorful ancestor, Edward Michael Elmore. Just thinking about how long ago the person lived was baffling to Edward. He would meet his grandmother's great-grandfather!

# 11

Edward Michael Elmore was a tall, dark-haired man with blue eyes and a beard that came to a point below his chin. He had extra-long fingers and an all-knowing smile that gave him a mysterious air, and the old-fashioned suit he wore looked as if it had been borrowed from a museum. His namesake told Edward that since they were both Edward Michael, Edward should call him Michael.

Edward did not comprehend why people from the South would have fought their relatives and friends in the North so that they could own slaves, but he enjoyed the tales of Michael's mindreading escapades, which included famous people like Abraham Lincoln. Michael told Edward that the president was intelligent but stubborn. President Lincoln refused to heed Michael's warnings to stay away from the play on the night that John Wilkes Booth shot him.

George Armstrong Custer was yet another historic figure who ignored Michael's advice. Michael had liked and admired Custer, though the man was insensitive to Native Americans.

In counseling prominent men and women of the time, Michael was usually given perks, like being treated to rooms in the finest hotels and meals in the best restaurants. Consequently, he wasn't wealthy, but he often hobnobbed with the upper class. It was on a business trip to Baltimore that he met Emily Peterson. Instantly, the two connected, and despite Michael's humble background, she agreed to marry him. They had a son they named Samuel, but Emily died in childbirth.

Settling down to raise Samuel, Michael lived out the rest of his life in Boston, where he lectured on what was a revolutionary topic for those times: self-improvement. All the while, he took care of Samuel, whom Michael said was a "good boy." He did not have his father's special talents, but Samuel became a talented writer and married Lucy Schuyler. Samuel and Lucy later had a son named Robert, and Robert's daughter was Edward's grandmother, Bernice.

Edward had no idea how long he had been with Michael, but when his ancestor departed, the child went to Miriam. "I met Michael," he said. "Well, he's really Edward Michael, but since we have the same name, I call him Michael. He told me all about the night that Honest Abe Lincoln got shot and how he tried to warn him not to go to that silly play."

She was stunned at what Edward said. "What else did Michael say?" she asked. Edward told her that Emily had died while having a baby, but Samuel was a nice boy who grew up to be a writer. Dumbfounded, Miriam simply nodded. It was way beyond her comprehension.

Michael continued to visit Edward in the company of Uriel, and they chose the backyard swing set as their place to meet. In addition to sharing stories about the past, Michael taught Edward how to develop his psychic gift. By learning to focus on the world around him, Edward enhanced his psychic abilities.

Paul and Miriam noted that Edward's awareness of the world around him was more acute, and whatever he was doing—Edward called them his "mental exercises"—was helping him overcome his Asperger's.

Before the school year was over, Edward asked his parents if he could spend the last two months at home focusing on his special work. "It's really important," he said. Seeing that this "work" was helping Edward, they agreed if their son completed everything his teacher assigned.

Edward, therefore, spent the rest of the spring and summer training with Michael. To practice his skills, Edward would invite the neighborhood children to his house. From Michael, he had learned how to engage others, so the kids loved being part of Edward's "games." Edward would either guess what was happening in each child's life or make a prediction about the future. His incredible accuracy amazed his friends, and some even offered to pay Edward. The boy, however, would not take their money. He simply enjoyed making them happy while being the center of attention.

Not surprisingly, the kids told their parents, which stirred up chatter, and eventually the media got wind of Edward's abilities. When three different local reporters called for interviews, Miriam and Paul got nervous. The last thing they wanted was their son to be classified as a freak. Paul used his prominence as an attorney to keep the reporters away, but he also exerted his parental influence over Edward.

"Son, you haven't done anything wrong, but your mother and I don't want you to play this game anymore," said Paul. "If you need to warn someone of danger, that's okay, but do it quietly. Let's draw the line there."

Edward obediently agreed. By honing his abilities and connecting with other children, he finally felt self-confident. He also felt that he had a real purpose in life, which was to help others—with or without using his psychic ability. Preferably, he would counsel others through the wisdom he gained from his spiritual guides.

"I'm excited about going back to school," Edward told his parents. He did not immediately tell them, however, that his new teacher was psychic

# 12

When his eighth birthday came along, Edward went with his parents to New York to be part of a live TV audience for a nationally broadcast children's program. Edward sat in the audience with one hundred other children for the production. Enthralled by all the behind-the-scenes activity, Edward could not get over the fact that indoor and outdoor scenery that seemed so solid and real was made of partitions that moved to create the sets. When the show went into a commercial, Edward observed the how various key people—makeup artists, the producer, and others—went into action with their roles.

A few weeks later in school, his teacher asked each student to share what he or she wanted to be as an adult. Edward, who had become enamored with the idea of appearing on television and becoming famous, did not want to sound boastful. Therefore, he sheepishly said that he wanted to be a policeman.

When class was over that day, Ms. Adams, psychic as well as attuned to her students, asked Edward to stay behind for a couple of minutes. She knew that Edward had not been honest in class, and she asked him why. Edward hesitated, but Ms. Adams told him that it was okay.

"You want to be rich and famous," she said. "I know, too, that you want to do good things for other people. Never be afraid to say what you truly feel or want."

When Edward went home that evening, he told his mother what Ms. Adams had said. "She was right," said Miriam. "Instead of being embarrassed, Edward, you should be happy that you know what you want in life."

When Michael appeared again to Edward, he told the boy that he should never lose sight of his dreams. "What you believe can happen is what will happen," said Michael. Those were Michael's parting words. It was time for Uriel to take over again as Edward's guide. As a tribute to his friend, Edward dressed up like Michael for Halloween. He wore a nineteenth century-style suit and hat. Miriam used an eyebrow pencil to give him a mustache. The neighborhood kids and adults told Edward he had the best costume.

Halloween and Thanksgiving came and went quickly that year for Paul and Miriam, though Christmas couldn't arrive quickly enough for Edward. The family had decided to take a trip to Disney World in Orlando, and in addition to seeing Mickey Mouse, Edward sensed something special about that part of Florida. As he would figure out, Orlando was a haven for psychics and psychic energy.

On this trip, Edward reminded his parents that he was not like most other eight-year-olds by asking if they could attend a psychic festival that weekend. Because they weren't like most parents, Miriam and Paul complied.

While at the festival, Edward witnessed a man reading cards for a young woman. The man was telling her that she would fall in love and marry a man within two years. Edward eyed the fortuneteller because the prediction was untrue. This young woman would be in a boating accident and die. He almost announced that the psychic was wrong, but Edward decided that it would be best to keep quiet.

Edward next overheard a woman telling an older man that his business was going to acquire a new contract that would make him a millionaire within five years. Again, Edward knew the fortune was not accurate. The man was going to have a heart attack within six months, followed by a stroke, and that he would be incapacitated for the rest of his life.

Why weren't the fortunetellers being truthful?

Edward asked his parents to wait a second while he approached the female psychic. The doomed man had already paid her and moved on. "Why didn't you tell him the truth?" he asked.

The psychic looked into Edward's eyes and realized that she wasn't answering to an ordinary child. "Child, it is often better to give people hope than to give them doom." Edward thought about this for a few minutes. He wasn't sure about lying, but maybe it would be better to give people some element of hope than not any at all. Perhaps, Edward thought, the psychics could have offered warnings. He might have cautioned the man to change his health habits. Maybe it was possible to change a person's fate.

This gave Edward plenty to think about, and he later asked Uriel what he might have done in that situation. Uriel told him that Edward would know what to say with each situation. For some, their fate was sealed; others could alter their lives by taking a different path. Edward would remember Uriel's words. If he planned to help people, Edward would use his heart to determine whom he could influence and whom he could not.

After leaving the fair, the Rippingtons decided to have a relaxing dinner at Epcot Center. They chose the Moroccan restaurant, and while waiting for a table, they browsed one of the nearby shops. When an unusual necklace caught Edward's eyes, a saleswoman explained that it was an amulet used to ward off evil spirits. The notion of an evil spirit puzzled Edward because he had only dealt with good spirits.

Still, Edward was curious and asked his father if he could have the piece of jewelry. At first, Paul said that it was unnecessary, but

Edward persisted. "If it means that much to you, okay," his dad said. Later, when Edward asked Uriel about the amulet, his spirit guide told the boy that he was right to follow his instincts and to wear it always for protection.

While they were dining, a young woman performed a belly dance. Edward told Paul and Miriam that she had just lost her father. Reminded once again of Edward's capabilities, Paul repeated to Edward how important it was for him to use his gift with care.

After dinner, the family strolled through the park, stopping by a futuristic exhibit. Edward liked the telephones with television monitors. When everyone had a TV phone, they would be able to see Edward's show, no matter where they happened to be.

That night, sleep came quickly and heavily. Edward dreamed about the day's activities and what he had learned. He had gathered a tremendous amount of information for use in the future. Edward also dreamed about the exotic dinner and the young belly dancer.

The remainder of their trip was filled with little boy fun at the Magic Kingdom. Edward met Mickey and Minnie Mouse, Donald Duck, Pluto, and Goofy. The Rippingtons rode nearly every ride and enjoyed the variety of performances. Edward couldn't wait to share his adventures with his classmates. He would tell them all about Epcot Center and Disney World, but he would keep the psychic fair visit to himself. Some things were best left unsaid.

# 13

As Edward learned to be more self-expressive, he viewed Valentine's Day with a new perspective. Taking care to decorate a box with a Cupid silhouette and hearts for all the valentines he would receive from his classmates, Edward also realized the significance of giving cards in exchange. He made a special effort on the valentines he designed for Ms. Adams, Billy, and Catherine.

Ms. Adams, in turn, had a one-of-a-kind card for Edward. "Always remember to go with your first instinct and stick to it," she wrote. She would do whatever was necessary to help Edward become the best that he could.

Ms. Adams gave all her students a variety of activities to stimulate their young minds. Thinking of a color, she asked the children to guess the one she had in mind and write it down. Edward was the only child to guess brown, the color she selected. (She expected Edward to know, but with twenty-eight kids in her class, Ms. Adams had thought that one or two others would get lucky.) She then asked the children to guess the animal she was thinking about, and Edward, again, was the one to pick an elephant, her choice.

Eager to expose her class to the world around them, Ms. Adams planned a fieldtrip to the Natural History Museum in New York City. Miriam volunteered as a chaperone, and their daytrip proceeded on schedule. Twenty miles into the excursion, however, Edward raised his hand for Ms. Adams' attention.

"Could we stop at the next exit?" he asked. "I don't want to have an accident."

"Honey, there's a restroom on the bus, so we don't need to stop," she said.

"No, I don't mean *that* kind of accident," Edward said. "There's going to be a car crash in a minute. We need to pull over."

Ms. Adams, too, had felt something was wrong, so she calmly asked the driver to get gas. He said that the tank was nearly full, but Ms. Adams insisted. He shrugged his shoulders, and said, "You're the boss."

If they had proceeded, Edward's bus would have been involved in a collision with seven other vehicles. The first and last were tractor-trailers, and the other cars were smashed in between. There were four fatalities and numerous injuries, and the highway was closed between the two exits for five hours. Edward's bus had to take a detour to return to the interstate.

The other children were informed that a little accident had occurred, but Edward knew the extent of it. Even though he was sad for the loss of lives, he sensed that the spirit souls were at peace. Besides, his interactions with Michael and Uriel made him unafraid of dying. He simply did not want to go before his time.

Realizing that there was no need to worry about the individuals who had lost their lives, Edward turned his total attention to the Museum of Natural History. His favorite exhibit displayed the woolly mammoth, reminding him of the elephant, which he loved. Sharing the joy of the children, Ms. Adams and Miriam also relaxed and took pleasure in the outing. The day proceeded without a hitch until it was time to leave. Ms. Adams did a headcount of the kids, but mistakenly counted one child twice. She didn't realize that Eve, a quiet, dark-headed child, was missing until Edward said so.

"She's at the information desk, crying," Edward said. Ms. Adams left the children with Miriam and the driver and ran back inside. Sure enough, there was Eve, crying, just as Edward had said. On the bus ride back home, everyone was chattering about Edward. They couldn't comprehend how he knew about Eve, but they sure were impressed!

During the weeks and months ahead, Edward's abilities strengthened and so did his confidence. In general, Edward was extremely bright, so Miriam and Paul decided that the family should use the summer vacation to broaden their son's experiences and feed his curious mind. They decided to visit Washington, Atlanta, Tampa, and New Orleans. "We'll head out West next year," Paul promised.

In Washington, DC, they stayed at the Mayflower Hotel, which was a grand old site of many inaugural balls. While in the area, the family would take tours of the White House, the Capitol Building, the Library of Congress, and the National Archives. Accompanying Edward were Uriel and Michael Elmore, who wanted to give his descendent an authentic understanding of American history.

On the White House tour, for instance, Michael reminded Edward that he had told President Lincoln not to go to the theater on the evening of the assignation. Mrs. Kennedy, the president's secretary, had also felt that something bad would happen, but the country's leader felt it was necessary to appear in public. "He wanted to demonstrate our nation's ability to heal after the Civil War by continuing to take part in normal activities," said Michael. Reflecting on the evening, he added, "I've often thought that if I could relive that night, I would handcuff the president to his chair to prevent him going to Ford's Theatre. The event, however, was destined to be; I was not meant to interfere beyond offering advice."

"Did lots of people not listen to you?" asked Edward. Michael said that about as many heeded his advice as those who did not, but he most regretted President Lincoln's decision.

Another day, a congressional assistant, Wendy Jenkins, gave the family a tour of the Senate and House of Representatives. Articulately explaining how laws were passed, Wendy observed Edward's intelligence and made certain she did not talk down to him.

"Did you enjoy the tour," she asked him at the end.

"It was really interesting," Edward smiled, turning beet-red. He had developed a crush on her, so Wendy gave him a goodbye kiss on the cheek. She also presented Edward with her business card. "If you're ever in DC, Edward, you should call me, okay?" Edward thought it was so cool that a beautiful grownup would go on a date with him, and he showed his gratitude with a big hug.

Later, while having dinner at an outdoor café with his parents, Edward seemed absorbed in the happenings between a man and woman at another table. "Edward, you shouldn't stare at other people," said Paul.

"I'm sorry," said Edward. "What is an affair? The man is having one. His wife is sad, but she's not the lady with him."

"Son, it's best not to pick up every bit of information from the people around you," said Paul. "People have a right to their privacy." Edward looked ashamed, so Miriam gave Paul a nudge under the table. "Don't worry," Paul added. "You meant well. You're still learning how to use your gift." Edward promised his father that he would not say anything else about people around them at dinner.

The following day, the family visited the National Archives in the morning and the Smithsonian Natural History Museum in the afternoon. Assuming that was enough touring for one day, Paul and Miriam planned to spend the evening at the hotel. Edward, however, wanted to see the Lincoln Memorial at night. Unable to take his eyes off the statue, Edward gazed at Lincoln's features until his head began to nod with fatigue. He had hoped to communicate with the president, but the boy did not feel the great man's presence. Barely able to keep his eyes open, Edward finally said he was willing to leave.

A trip to George Washington's Mount Vernon home was a bit more spirited. Among all the rooms in the mansion, Washington's study proved to be Edward's favorite. Edward was drawn to the many fascinating history books on the shelves as well as to General Washington's presence. When mentally acknowledging the great man, however, Edward learned that the country's first president preferred to be known as General Washington, not President Washington. Being head of a country felt too much like having the title and power of a king.

That was, perhaps, the most significant insight Edward gained from his trip to DC.

# 14

After the long days of sightseeing in DC, the Rippingtons slowed their pace on their drive to Atlanta. They could have made it in one exhausting day of travel, but the family leisurely drove it in three days with numerous stops along the way.

Though they stayed in a hotel, the Rippingtons planned to visit Randy and Debbie Walker, cousins of Miriam's father. The Walkers had never met Edward, but they had heard much about the remarkable boy. Randy was especially excited to meet Edward. As it turned out, he had a severe gambling problem, and owing the local bookies about thirty thousand dollars, Randy wanted to see if Edward could change his fate by predicting the winners of the day's baseball games.

Instead of meeting the Rippingtons for dinner, Randy insisted that the threesome come to their house for a barbecue. Miriam had brought an old scrapbook that once belonged to her grandfather, Robert Walker. Robert's brother, Philip Walker, had been an alcoholic and a gambler. Because of Philip's problems, Robert Walker had kept his distance from his brother. When Miriam's dad Stan was growing up, he had known very little about his Uncle Philip or Philip's son (and Stan's first cousin) Marty. It wasn't until Marty was in college that he and Stan had become friendly.

Marty, fortunately, did not take after his father; sharp and diligent, he became a successful entrepreneur and owner of several businesses. Nevertheless, the gambling gene resurfaced in Marty's son.

Randy had lost most of his inherited fortune gambling. Though he and his wife lived in a grand, southern mansion on five acres of land, the property was heavily mortgaged. Without saying so, Paul and Miriam both noted that portions of the grounds appeared to need tending, but they might have assumed that summer rains had caused an abundance of weeds, challenging even the most impeccably kept landscapes.

Diverting Edward from the group, Randy tossed him a rubber ball and asked if he like to play catch in the pool. He was plotting to build a rapport with his little cousin. After a bit, Randy asked Edward if he liked baseball, to which Edward replied, "I like it, but I'm not good enough to be on a team." Randy then asked if Edward had a favorite team, which presented an opportunity to talk about the sport. Randy proceeded by pulling out a newspaper and showing Edward that the Braves were playing the Giants that night. Trying to sound casual, he asked Edward who he thought would win. Edward looked at the paper and said that the Giants would win. Masking his enthusiasm, Randy proceeded to go through the other games of the day, and Edward picked a winner for each.

With his betting list confirmed, Randy excused himself to call his bookie. When he returned in a million-dollar mood, he invited the crew to that night's Braves' game. The Rippingtons accepted, and Randy couldn't wait to see Edward's predictions come true.

Every aspect of the crowded stadium was a thrill to Edward. He loved the smell of peanuts and hotdogs, the echoing enthusiasm of the announcer on the public-address system, and the sight of the confident players jogging onto the field. He didn't care who won. Just being there live was a treat!

Neither team, however, scored during the first inning. Randy, a bit nervous, asked Edward what he thought the final score would be. He made certain no one else overheard him ask such a question. Edward replied that the Giants would win five to three, so Randy tried to relax. When the Giants were behind two to zero after six innings, Randy was sweating. Had he made a mistake by listening to this kid? He was feeling a bit hopeful when the Giants scored one run at the top of the seventh, but the Braves scored again in the bottom.

Randy leaned over to Edward and quietly asked, "Are you still sure of the score?" Edward assured him that Uriel was always right.

"Who is Uriel?" It was all Randy could do to refrain from grabbing Edward by the shoulders and shaking him.

Edward replied that Uriel was best friend. "He's right behind you."

Randy quickly looked around to see three empty seats. "There is no one behind us," Randy whispered to Edward. Trying to control his voice, Randy asked Paul, "Have you ever heard of Uriel?"

"Oh, so Edward's told you about his guardian angel, has he?" Paul replied.

Boiling with fury, Randy wanted to strangle the kid. He bought himself a beer and gulped it down. He was contemplating if he could climb to some high point and jump to his death when the crowed started booing and cheering. The eighth inning began with the Giants' shortstop walking. A long fly ball to right field by the second baseman followed. The Giants' catcher then hit into a double play, and the side was retired. The Braves went down one, two, three in the bottom of the eighth. Randy was suddenly alive with the score, now three to one.

The pitcher led off the ninth inning for the Giants and grounded out. With only two outs left, Randy left for a bathroom break, resigned to the fact that he was stupid to have listened to the kid. He may as well flush the twenty bucks he had left to his name in the toilet!

While he was gone, the Giants' first baseman singled to right, followed by a walk to the third baseman. The left fielder hit a popup just past the infield for the second out. Then the right fielder hit a single to short centerfield. The bases were now loaded, and Randy was nowhere in sight. The right fielder took the first two pitches, a strike and a ball. The next pitch was fouled off behind the backstop. The pitch after that was a ball, low and inside. It was now a full count with only one pitch left in the game, but it was fouled out just to the right of the flagpole. The right fielder fouled the next two pitches out of play. The final pitch was a curveball that the right fielder tagged straight to center and out of the park for a grand slam. Miraculously, the Giants won five to three!

Assuming the cheers were for the Braves, Randy slumped back into his seat. That's why he didn't believe his eyes when he saw the right fielder crossing the plate. Astounded, he glanced at the scoreboard, which placed him in a near state of shock. At the same time, it occurred to him that six other games had been completed. The scoreboard, flashing the results of the other games, confirmed that Edward had picked all the winners. Only three games remained in play on the West Coast.

Animated once again, Randy talked incessantly in the car on the way to the Rippington's hotel. Somehow, Edward had managed to fall asleep, but Miriam and Paul were rather relieved to say goodnight. As they pulled away from the hotel, Debbie asked Randy, "What has you so hyper tonight?"

"Oh, I'm just glad that Edward had such a good time at the game." Unaware of the win-or-lose-everything bets her husband had placed, Debbie went to bed while Randy stayed up well past midnight, waiting for the West Coast game results.

Wired from the previous night's victories, Randy barely slept. He forced himself to wait until nine in the morning before calling the Rippingtons. "Let me take you around sightseeing today," he offered. Miriam and Paul graciously accepted.

Randy, who was extremely anxious to spend a little alone time with Edward, didn't think the boy had a clue about the gambling. He was wrong. Edward had consulted Uriel, who explained that gambling was a problem, an illness that cannot easily be cured. Uriel had warned Edward that helping his cousin win enough to recover his losses would not end the trouble. "Randy won't be able to avoid the temptation of gambling," Uriel advised. "He'll want you to predict the outcome of more games."

They had a moment to themselves during lunch when Randy offered to take Edward to the restaurant's gift shop before the waiter brought their orders. As soon as they were away from the parents' view, Randy asked Edward to make his selections. Noting that his cousin did not ask him to pick winners, Edward picked each game's losing team. Assuming he would double his money, Randy immediately called his bookie to bet every penny he had won the day before.

That would be the last time that Edward or anyone would hear from Randy. The Rippingtons left the next day for Tampa. Randy left to start a new life as Walker Edwards. He owed some scary people a fearful amount of money.

# 15

While heading down the interstate to Tampa, more precisely to St. Petersburg, Uriel explained that Randy's greed would have destroyed him. His cousin's only hope was to turn his life around as Walker Edwards. He wanted Edward to remember that lesson.

Edward would acquire additional insights while visiting St. Petersburg. The Rippingtons were following the recommendation of Roald Dahl, who suggested taking Edward to the old city because of its spiritual significance. Local grounds once belonged to the Tocobaga Indians, a tribe that had flourished there for centuries. They had blessed the area to ward off hurricanes, and to this day, St. Petersburg has never had a direct hit from one.

After the first Spaniards arrived on the coastal spot in 1528, the Tocobaga Indians died out, partly from the diseases they caught from the Europeans and partly from the battles that ensued. Consequently, although the Tocobaga were rather peaceful, their burial mounds were what primarily remained of them. Uriel not only told Edward that he would contact some of the tribal spirits, but the boy would also one day settle in the area.

After the hectic pace of DC and Atlanta, the Rippingtons were happy to slow things down. Paul had reserved a room at a fine old hotel on St. Petersburg Beach. Exquisitely understated, their room contained mahogany antique furniture, white walls and bedding, and original paintings in pastel hues. No one had trouble drifting off to sleep on their first night.

The family spent the next morning on the beach before touring the town. On Park Street, a sign indicated where Pánfilo de Narváez, a Spanish explorer, had first landed in Florida. Interested in learning more history, they visited a museum that housed numerous relics from the period. Along with the artifacts were several Indian and Spanish spirits who had never crossed over into the light.

Edward gathered the spirits into a group and explained that they needed to cross over. In response, they told Edward that they were there to protect the area. Edward, however, persisted, explaining that it was time for them to move on. Though other people had tried to help the spirits cross in the past, Edward was the first to be successful.

After the crossing, the museum's curator shared that the museum had been haunted since it was first built. Among many unusual happenings, like lights flickering for no reason and books falling off shelves without anyone nearby, certain spots in the museum would drop ten or more degrees in temperature for short periods of time. When the curator finished, Edward said, "You won't be having any more of that happening here."

The gentleman smiled without realizing the boy was telling the truth. In the uneventful weeks and months that followed, however, the curator wondered if that child had sent the spirits away. Paul and Miriam did not ask Edward what had happened, but their instincts told them their son had used his powers in a positive way.

Proceeding to downtown St. Petersburg for more sightseeing, the Rippingtons enjoyed the nostalgic old buildings and tropical setting. Parking by an old apartment building, Paul informed his family that Babe Ruth had lived there during spring training with the New York Yankees. A smooth-talking attorney, Paul convinced the building manager to let them see number 702. The manager provided some historical tidbits. "Babe's housekeeper talked him out of committing suicide in here," the man said. Edward immediately sensed overwhelming fear and asked his parents if they could leave.

Their next stop was a park near Tampa Bay. Uriel said that Tampa would grow significantly and would one day have pro baseball, football, and hockey teams. Edward happily anticipated attending lots of baseball games when he moved there.

The following day, Edward pretended to be surprised when his father announced that they would be visiting Ybor City. Edward smiled because Uriel had prepared him. They crossed a long bridge that stretched for miles from St. Petersburg to Tampa. Because he loved the water, Edward felt he was in paradise.

Tampa, like St. Pete, had a definite Spanish influence. Taking in the culture, the family chose a Cuban restaurant in Ybor City to have their lunch before exploring the area. Edward was fascinated with the numerous fortunetelling shops, though Uriel said that Edward's talents were far more acute.

Edward spotted a man nearby. Though his attire was unremarkable—leather sandals, blue shorts, a striped navy shirt, and baseball cap—the man seemed odd. He glanced at Edward and nodded, then disappeared. Uriel told Edward that he was seeing into the future and that the man was Edward! One day, Uriel said that Edward would hone this ability to the point at which looking into the future would seem as natural as the present.

"Time," Uriel explained, "is nonexistent in the way most humans perceive. The past, present, and future all exist simultaneously."

Edward was baffled, but Uriel tried to explain that several dimensions existed. "Each one overlaps the other," Uriel said. Edward still did not understand. "An area of knowledge called quantum physics will help you grasp this phenomenon when you are older.

You will study quantum physics and gain a mastery of the subject." Edward put this information in the back of his head for later use.

With so much weighing on his brain, Edward was eager to go swimming. The clear, aqua waters of the Gulf of Mexico enticed many, but they especially attracted Edward. He was as close to heaven as he could imagine.

While floating in the water, Edward spotted two bottle-nosed dolphins nearby. He instinctively felt a connection to them, and the mammals felt free to communicate with him through visual telepathy. They showed Edward an ancient land which they called Atlantis. They conveyed that a tidal wave had flooded the city thousands of years ago. Though most of its inhabitants had drowned, a few hundred were swept into an underground cave. They swam through a passage to another cave that opened into a larger cave full of oxygen and fluorescent light. The survivors and their descendants made the magical place home for several thousand years. While some remained in the cave, others adapted to underwater breathing, evolving into what became known as mer-people, or people of the sea.

Other Atlanteans migrated to the land of Sumeria, where they built cities. The third largest of these cities was called Ur, the home of a young boy named Avram. Avram's father was an idol maker, but the boy grew up believing in one supreme energy. Unable to live among his people, Avram left Sumeria. He changed his name to Abraham, took two wives, and had two sons by them. Ishmael, the elder son, had children who started the Moslem religion. Yitzhak, the second son, had twelve sons who became the twelve tribes of Israel. Yitzhak became Israel after wrestling with an angel, and through Israel's son Yakov, the Jewish people emerged. This was the beginning of two of the world's major religions of ancient times.

That part of the telepathic movie seemed to take hours, and Edward broke away for a moment. He was surprised that only a matter of minutes had passed, so he asked the dolphins to proceed. They obliged, showing Edward that beings from other galaxies had visited Earth over thousands of years. The dolphins informed Edward that some of the beings were still on Earth to help the Atlanteans sustain their way of life.

Before the dolphins swam away, they let Edward know that they would always be there, whenever he needed them. They also transferred their ability to communicate telepathically to Edward; he could, therefore, read other people's thoughts. Though he wanted to tell Miriam and Paul about what had occurred, Uriel advised him to wait until a more appropriate time. When it was time to leave, Edward reluctantly left the water. He would never forget that experience.

Dreaming that evening, Edward was with the dolphins. Suddenly, a sand shark began swimming toward him. The dolphins swam to a position between the shark and Edward. As the shark came closer, the dolphins moved in and the shark retreated.

When he went swimming the next day, Edward once again attracted the dolphins. Approaching him within inches, the dolphins told Edward that his dream was real. They would protect Edward from evil. He should also not be fearful of the day when a great tidal wave washed all of Florida underwater. That day would be many years into the future, as would the day when he would move into the next dimension.

After making their promise, the dolphins would prove that their words were true. A nine-foot sand shark was swimming directly towards Edward. The dolphins turned and forced the shark out to deep waters. Watching Edward from the shore, Paul and Miriam were frantically running towards their son. When they reached him, Edward assured them that he was all right. "The dolphins protected me," he said. Paul and Miriam, however, had had enough excitement for one day. It was time to travel on to New Orleans.

# 16

Upon arriving in New Orleans, Edward encountered several ghosts. A finely attired lady of the 1800s and a bellman of the same century attempted to make conversation. Edward tried to ignore them, but when a man and woman in his room said that he was there to solve their murders, they had his attention.

"*What* do you want me to do?" Edward had never heard such a request.

The male spirit proceeded with introductions. "We are Michel and Corinne Rousseau." Vacationing in New Orleans thirty years ago, the couple had come from France for Mardi Gras. Returning to their hotel one evening, a man with a gun approached and forced them into an alley. He robbed and then shot them both twice, once in the chest and once in the stomach. They were discovered in the alley a few hours later.

Corinne described the man as about six feet tall and weighing approximately two hundred fifty pounds. He had blue eyes, black hair, and a tattoo on his left hand. "It was an anchor wrapped with a snake," she said. Their murderer, Leon Dupree, lived nearby with his daughter and granddaughter.

"What can I do?" Edward asked. The spirits conveyed that Leon's daughter would be wearing Corinne's necklace, the sign of Virgo encrusted with sapphires. Like Edward, Corrine's birthday was September thirteenth, as the pendant's zodiac sign and birthstone signified. To prove it was hers, their daughter Ornella had a picture of Corinne wearing the necklace. Ornella, who had been only two when her parents were murdered, moved to New Orleans as an adult. "She will not get on with her life until the crime against us is resolved," said Corrine.

The plan was for Edward to tell his parents, who could help him contact Ornella and provide her with the necessary information. Since Paul was the attorney in the family, he called Ornella. He couldn't say that his son talked to her parents' spirits, so he simply offered to help her solve their murders. Ornella was slightly skeptical, but they arranged to meet in the hotel's café. Paul also asked her to bring her mother's picture with her.

Edward recognized her immediately, as Ornella had dark, curly hair and olive complexion like her mother. She entered the cafe with an air of distinction that also resembled Corinne. Now a writer, the author had published a few bestsellers about real murders; she was one to ask probing questions. Meeting the attorney and his family, she was anxious to learn what possible news they could possess regarding her parents.

Determining that they needed to present the truth in a straightforward, professional manner, Paul revealed Edward's special abilities. She listened intently, but Ornella did not demonstrate any emotion until Edward quietly said, "Your parents want to tell you that they are proud of you." At that point, she began to cry.

After writing down the facts, Ornella decided to contact a detective on the police force named Harry Dawson. From researching her books, she and Harry had established a friendly connection. In fact, because of his friendship and respect for Ornella, Harry agreed to meet the group as soon as she called him.

Harry had worked with psychics in the past, but he was amazed that a boy as young as Edward could relate such clear-cut information. "The psychics I know get cloudy pictures in their minds or certain feelings that can be helpful, but never has one been so specific," Harry said

When they were finished, Harry promised to pay a call on the daughter and Leon. He took the picture of Corinne wearing the unique necklace. Ornella thanked Harry as he left. Harry said, "The one to thank is Edward!"

Ornella then expressed her gratitude to the Rippingtons. She would let them know about any developments in the case.

The next morning, Harry informed Ornella that Leon Dupree had been shot while attempting to flee from the police. He was in the hospital, recovering from his wounds before being transferred to jail. They had recovered her mother's necklace, which she would receive after the trial. Dupree's daughter had no idea where Leon had gotten the necklace and was horrified to know that her father had killed Ornella's parents.

Ornella called Paul to let him know what had taken place. He assumed they would go about their vacation as usual, but as the Rippingtons left their hotel, a crowd of reporters wanted to know about Edward. Someone, not Harry, in the department had tipped off the press. Harry arrived just in time to escort the family to police headquarters for a debriefing. Paul and Miriam were happy to comply; they would do anything to avoid the mob outside the hotel.

On the way to the police station, Harry asked if Edward would like to help with another current investigation. "That is, young man, if your parents say it's okay." Miriam and Paul only wanted to be sure that Edward was comfortable with the idea. Edward, it seemed, was thrilled to help.

The case involved a woman found dead in her apartment. She had been slashed five times with a kitchen knife. Oddly, the door was locked and bolted from the inside, and she lived alone. There were no witnesses to the crime. "The person who did that is dead," Edward said.

"How do you know that?" Harry asked.

"Her name is Yvonne Wolper, right?" Edward asked. "She's here with us now."

Harry almost ran off the road, so he pulled over to hear the rest of what the boy had to offer.

"She was dabbling in voodoo," Edward said. "It got out of hand. That's all she'll tell me for now, but Yvonne does not want you to dig into her case."

"Well, thanks, son," said Harry. He decided to leave the boy alone. It was probably too much to expect a kid to get involved in such gory business. Harry made sure they finished up the questioning quickly and then helped the Rippingtons check out of the hotel and leave town without fanfare. Once again, he thanked Edward and his parents, and wished them well.

By late afternoon, the Rippingtons were on the highway. Before going home, they would be stopping in Birmingham. Paul had a meeting there with Arty Robinson, the same Arty who had been part of the group the night Miriam and Paul met. Arty, a Civil Rights attorney, apparently had an intriguing proposition for Paul. Edward, who was learning to see the past and future more clearly, knew all about the proposition. Arty would offer Paul a lucrative partnership in his firm. While Miriam would be reluctant to leave her practice in Hartford, the family would move to Birmingham.

# 17

Birmingham, a city nestled in the foothills of the Appalachian Mountains, appealed to Edward, but he looked forward to the time when St. Petersburg would be his home. While in Alabama, he would make many friends and solve numerous murder crimes, yet he had so much more to accomplish later in life.

Though Miriam was not keen on relocating from Hartford, she warmed up to the city. The people, ready to extend Southern hospitality, were friendly, and the location was beautiful. The area had a fascinating history as well. Birmingham, once a steel producing center that had transformed itself to an educational one, was well-known for its fine medical and law schools. Both Miriam and Paul had eventually wanted to teach part-time, so the opportunity certainly existed here.

The Rippingtons moved in time for Edward to begin the new school year in Birmingham. Quickly making friends, he wanted to invite his entire class to celebrate his thirteenth birthday. He especially wanted to include Tammy Vandergraf. He had a crush on the girl for several reasons. She was not only smart, but Edward could not take his eyes off her thick auburn hair and cat-green eyes. The Vandergrafs and Rippingtons lived only minutes apart, so the families started getting together for barbecues and potluck dinners.

For his birthday, Edward received a camera and a puppy. The

puppy was a fawn-colored male boxer that Edward named Rusty. The pair became like best friends. If neither answered when called, the two could be found in the spacious backyard playing toss and fetch with a tennis ball. Often, Tammy wandered over to join them.

Edward, who was funny, smart, and friendly, became popular in school and among the neighborhood kids. A natural leader, he began writing short stories and plays, and then assigning and directing kids to take part in various roles. They would gather after school to practice and then perform for their parents on Saturdays.

Having become less constrained by the normal concept of time, Edward was still surprised by how quickly the summer arrived. His parents had purchased a beach cottage in Panama City, Florida, and he took advantage of his opportunities to swim with the dolphins. One would allow him to take hold of a fin as they darted through the warm Gulf of Mexico waters. People walking along the beach would often stop in amazement if they spotted Edward with one of his sea pals. *Is that boy really on a dolphin's back?*

From the shoreline, Rusty would bark frantically. The dog wasn't so sure about the arrangement! Miriam and Paul, however, permitted Edward to go because their son had become such a strong swimmer. Remembering a time when they wondered if he might not walk, they wouldn't dream of prohibiting him from experiencing something so exhilarating.

Edward had grown into a tanned, healthy boy. Tammy, who also vacationed in Panama City with her parents, clearly appreciated Edward's fine looks, and he liked hers.

One afternoon, Tammy asked Edward if he would kiss her. At first, Edward was nervous, but he quickly took to the notion and planted a soft, warm kiss on her lips. Edward felt a tingly feeling all over his body. He also got the same kind of goose bumps that occurred when something clicked in his head as verification that his instincts were right. He knew that he shared a deep spiritual connection with Tammy. They had to have known each other in a past life. Tammy liked Edward's kiss so much that she kissed him again. They both stepped back for a moment and stared curiously at each other.

Tammy asked, "Did you feel that?" Edward knew what she meant, and he answered, "Yes, I did. It was remarkable." They both smiled and hugged with a passion that they would both never forget. They truly were soulmates. Edward knew that he could tell Tammy anything, but he would wait.

Later that same afternoon, Tammy was running in the yard when she fell. A stick pierced the skin under her eye. Her mother took her to the emergency room, where Tammy received four stitches to close the wound. Her eye was black for several days, so children at school asked her what had happened. Tammy just laughed. The event was nothing because the encounter with Edward had been so special to her.

The two grew extremely close. On one occasion, out of the blue, Tammy asked Edward to dance with her. For some unknown reason, Edward said no. Hurt, Tammy said she needed to go home. Edward immediately offered to dance with her, but Tammy said that it was too late.

Edward was extremely upset about the incident because he did not realize it was not his fault. Asperger's syndrome, the mild autism he had, sometimes made him withdraw from others physically. If he could change anything, this would be it because similar situations would recur over his life.

# 18

By the end of the school year, Edward and Tammy reconciled. Tammy's mother had explained Edward's mild autism to her daughter, and once she understood, Tammy approached him with a new sense of compassion and felt closer to Edward than ever.

Their parents had become close, which led Tammy's parents to purchase a vacation home in Panama City as well. The kids, therefore, spent their summers together. Edward and Tammy loved to play on the beach with Rusty. For hours they would throw a rubber ball for Rusty to catch. Rusty, being a smart dog, would take turns delivering the ball to Tammy and Edward. When Rusty was tired, he would drop the ball and plop onto the sand.

On one such afternoon, the sky was growing dark with grey clouds, so Edward told Tammy he would walk her to her house and then take Rusty the rest of the way home. They would meet later after the brewing storm passed.

Halfway to his family's cottage, Edward noticed two men dressed in khaki slacks and polo shirts who seemed to be headed towards him. *Why are they dressed like that on the beach?* To be safe, Edward attempted to read their thoughts.

One of the men was focused on kidnapping Edward. Frightened, he felt his heart beating like crazy, but said, "Rusty, go!" Rusty ran ahead and approached the men from behind. The dog knocked one man down and growled, as if daring the other to take one step closer to Edward. Edward ran home while the men tried to back away from Rusty.

Breathless, Edward charged into the house, telling his mother to call the police. Edward then ran to the front window. He could see two small figures running in the opposite direction. Rusty, thankfully, was coming towards Edward. By the time the police arrived, the men were nowhere to be found. Without saying so to the police, Edward and Miriam knew that the strangers were interested in Edward's special abilities.

Edward, however, gave the police a complete description of the two men, which astoundingly included their names and where they were staying. The police asked Edward how he knew all this. Edward simply said that he had heard them talking. He didn't want to stir up controversy by telling the police that he had read their minds. Within a few hours, local law enforcement officers had located the men.

Though they were questioned, the suspects revealed nothing. Without evidence, other than a boy's belief that he was to be kidnapped, the police could not hold the men. Strangely, however, the same two men were killed in freak car accident that night. For no apparent reason, the driver seemed to lose control of his vehicle, a produce truck. The intended kidnappers' car had run into the truck, filled with watermelons, which came smashing through their windshield. The truck driver was unharmed, but the men in the car died of head trauma.

Because of the attempted kidnapping, Paul and Miriam took Edward back to Birmingham. Despite Edward's pleas that everything was all right, he had to leave Tammy. He wished he could stay with her but decided she would probably be safer without him around.

At the end of August, Tammy came knocking on the Rippingtons' door. "It wasn't any fun being at the beach without you," she told Edward. He understood and kissed her.

# 19

In eighth grade, Edward and Tammy had more homework with papers to write in addition to extra studying. They often worked side by side, blocking out the rest of the world as if no one else existed.

Plenty, however, was happening around them. Paul and Arty, for instance, took on a heated case involving the Ku Klux Klan. They were defending two African-American men who were on trial for beating a Klan member who had purportedly set both of their houses on fire. The violent case caused uproar among the citizens of Birmingham with protests that often ended in arrests.

One evening at dinner, Paul relayed facts about the trial. Tammy and Edward listened to him explain the sympathies and prejudices that ran deep on both sides. Paul and Arty began receiving threats at work and at home, so Paul and Miriam had decided to send Edward to stay with Miriam's parents up north. Edward didn't want to leave, but Paul assured him that it would be only until the trial was over.

The trial lasted three weeks, and Paul and Arty won their case, but they had made many angry, especially the KKK. Paul and Miriam, therefore, asked her parents to keep Edward until the end of the school year. The day after confirming the plan, Stan and Bernice got the news of a firebombing of the Rippingtons' home.

The bodies of Paul and Miriam had been identified. Arty, too, was also found dead.

Edward refused to believe the news. Uriel tried to console him, but the boy could not accept the facts. The worst part was that Edward had not foreseen the event. Why hadn't he? Had he been too distracted because he missed Tammy? If he had been more attuned to his parents, perhaps he would have perceived the danger and forewarned them. If Edward accepted this, he would have to face the fact that he had failed to protect his own parents. His life was turned upside down.

Wanting to do what was best for their grandson, Stan and Bernice decided that they should move to Birmingham. They hoped that by allowing Edward to return to his school and friends, he would pull out of his depression.

Of all people, Tammy was the only one who got through to Edward. She promised she would always be there for him.

With plenty of insurance money as well as the estate Paul and Miriam left behind, Stan and Bernice rebuilt the family's home. They held off moving to Alabama until construction was complete, so Edward never saw the destruction, nor did he want to see it. Despite his mental abilities, his protective subconscious blocked any visions before his conscious mind perceived them.

During the construction period, Stan and Bernice took Edward to the beach. Having a somewhat normal summer with Tammy helped Edward get through the trauma. He also had Rusty, who had escaped the fire.

The typical summer routine of swimming, playing ball with Rusty, and just being there with Tammy was especially critical to Edward. Like most who suffer with Asperger's syndrome, Edward depended on a familiar schedule.

Once back in Birmingham, Edward eased into daily life. School would soon start, so he had plenty of errands and shopping to do with his grandparents in preparation. Even so, he spent as many free moments as possible with Tammy. On one afternoon, he asked his grandparents to let Tammy and him stay at home while they went to buy notebook paper, pens, and other school supplies. Realizing he needed a break, Stan and Bernice agreed. While they were gone, the doorbell rang. Out of caution, Edward looked out and saw two men dressed in black suits and hats to match. Both were wearing sunglasses.

Edward suddenly began to have all kinds of visions flashing through his head. He was overwhelmed because the men were from the government and they had come for Edward.

Edward whispered to Tammy that they had to leave immediately by the back door. "Be quiet," he said. "We're going to your house."

Once at Tammy's, Edward told her what he knew. Against her protests, he told Tammy that he was going back home. "They are about to come here," he said. "When you say I'm not here, you'll be telling the truth." Edward slipped out and backtracked home. By the time he arrived, Bernice and Stan were back. They informed Edward that two men from the government were just there.

"I know," Edward said. Not knowing where to turn, they sat quietly, wishing that Edward would come up with a solution. As if on cue, the doorbell rang once again.

# 20

Before he had a chance to figure out what was happening, Edward was the passenger in a black sedan. The two agents were taking him to a secret facility outside Huntsville. This building had been used for the Monarch Butterfly Project, also known as MK-Ultra. It had been developed by Nazi German scientists who were brought to Huntsville, Alabama, after World War II to build rockets and conduct mind-control tests on American civilians.

The building had partially closed when the government moved most of its operations to Branson, Missouri, to be near a country music park. Though it seemed unbelievable to Edward, he had begun to perceive an array of extraordinary details. Apparently, many country singers had been unwittingly brainwashed as part of a covert drug operation. With government funds and a billionaire who owned a giant retail chain based in Arkansas, the country singers were being used as drug mules to transport narcotics around the world to undermine selected societies. Edward wondered how people who were sworn to uphold the Constitution could become involved in such despicable actions.

Once they reached their destination, the government agents began running all types of tests on Edward. The scientists confirmed that Edward was psychic. They reported that he could see dead people and read minds. Their tests had limitations, however;

they did not uncover anything about Uriel. Edward was physically and emotionally shaken, but he calmed down when Uriel told him to be patient; everything would be all right. Edward took a deep breath and began to relax.

Left locked in a room with six-inch metal walls for several hours, Edward almost laughed because he could read the minds of the scientists in the next room. Those guys thought they could block his senses with metal? The only thing that kept him from feeling smug was their intention to hook electrodes to his brain.

Edward was led down a corridor to a sterile operating room. On the way, he saw a framed portrait of a mustached man with dark, slicked-back hair. "Josef Mengele" was inscribed on a brass plate nailed to its frame. There were portraits of respected scientists as well, such as Albert Einstein and geneticist Gregor Mendel. Even so, Edward sensed that the room had been used for biological tests on soldiers and civilians. The scientists told Edward to lie on the table and relax. Relax? Were they kidding? Edward was beginning to panic, but he followed Uriel's advice to do as they said. That was the only way to get through the tests.

Uriel had also told Edward to let his mind wander. Edward instinctively knew that he must keep his thoughts from going to anything that could be used to aid in the scientists' attempt to read his mind. Edward began to do multiplication tables in his head, over and over. He was not that great at math, and usually had to count when multiplying by thirteen. This time, he went through the calculations flawlessly. Uriel, he realized, was feeding him the numbers. That knowledge helped him calm down. He was determined to get through the tests without revealing any additional information.

After the tests, Edward was led to another room that looked like a college dorm. Someone in a lab coat told him to lie down, take a nap. Reluctantly, Edward sat on the bed. Uriel told Edward to take a nap, and he would protect him. Exhausted, Edward gave in. He knew that Uriel would be there for him.

When the same person in the lab coat woke up Edward, the boy had no idea what time it was. There were no clocks anywhere. The man had brought Edward some dinner. Edward sensed that the food was not drugged, so he ate. He was starving. When he finished, he was led to room with a conference table. He was seated on one side and a panel of scientists sat across from him. They asked him all kinds of questions. Uriel told him how to answer each one, and Edward did so.

After answering one intense question after another, he felt like he had run a marathon. Edward calculated that about three hours of grilling had passed. The scientists excused him to go to bed, and Edward was grateful. He would rest now, worry later. Tomorrow, they had cautioned, would be a busy day.

Edward awoke with a start. He could not tell the time of day with no sunlight or moonlight as a gauge. The room, in fact, was black. Blinking his eyes so they could adjust to the dark, Edward was startled to see two creatures standing over him. He nearly jumped from the bed, but the beings began to communicate with him telepathically. They conveyed that they were extraterrestrials yet closely connected to the dolphins that Edward had met in St. Petersburg. The creatures showed him how they had come to Earth centuries before. During the Civil War, the creatures standing before Edward had established contact with his ancestor Edward Michael Elmore and helped him develop his powers. They were going to help Edward do the same.

By the way, they added, they had been in contact with another young boy many years ago. The child had average intelligence at first, but with their help, the young German was a genius. His name was Albert Einstein. Edward suddenly connected the dots and understood the reason for the portraits.

Between the scientists' experiments and the extraterrestrials' training, Edward came to realize that he had an important role to play in the world. He had the freedom to choose good or evil. His actions could benefit all of humankind, or he could fulfill his own personal desires. With his capabilities came powerful decisions and tremendous responsibility.

When they deemed it was time, the beings took Edward to a large hangar. It could have contained a fighter jet, but it held a huge metallic disc almost the size of Edward's house. A set of stairs led into the object, and Edward was ordered to climb them. It was an aircraft of some sort, Edward realized, as the creatures helped him strap himself into a cockpit chair. The two beings took their places, secured the straps, and proceeded to push a series of blinking buttons. Immediately, the ship began to dematerialize.

Within minutes, the ship rematerialized in another hangar. This one, however, was ten billion miles from Earth. The ladder engaged, and the two creatures and Edward disembarked. What was happening?

Approximately fifty creatures greeted them. The Xzanthians had lion heads and their bodies were covered in various tattoos that were symbols of a spiritual nature. Edward learned that their heads inspired the Sphinx in Egypt. The word *Sphin*, not coincidentally, was an Xzanthian name for their first leader. Telepathically, the current Xzanthian leader named Shabalai showed Edward that they had transported people from Earth to their planet in the same manner for thousands of years. Among the souls who had gone before Edward were Elijah and Moses. Elijah remained for decades, but Moses went back to lead his people. Incidentally, he departed and returned to Earth from Mount Sinai. Then, when the Israelites thought he had died, Moses returned to this planet. In fact, he wrote many of the laws that Joshua passed along as the new leader of the Israelites.

Edward spent six years on this planet, learning and developing his abilities. His instruction involved mental telepathy, mind reading, and healing. He was taught the ways of living a peaceful life and helping others.

When the creatures took Edward to Earth, they left him in Birmingham. His grandmother was shocked when she answered the door to find Edward standing there.

They embraced and cried, then talked for hours. In the best way he could, Edward provided an overview of his experiences. Though she was astounded, Bernice seemed to accept the facts in a pragmatic manner. She always believed that her grandson would serve an important purpose on Earth.

In turn, Bernice informed Edward that his grandfather had died three years earlier of heart failure. Edward reflected a moment before asking about Tammy. Bernice told Edward that she was about to graduate from the University of Alabama in Tuscaloosa. At that point, Edward had heard everything that he needed to know. He wasted no time obtaining driver's license and then went to buy a car. He was going to see Tammy.

Edward located Tammy at her dorm. Seeing him, she began to cry. She asked him where he had been, and Edward replied that he had been out of the country. He said that he had been waiting until it was safe to return.

The two became reacquainted. Talking about their desires and dreams, Edward said he wanted to earn a college degree. Tammy helped arrange a meeting with the dean of admissions, who interviewed Edward. Hearing that he had been on the run but continued his learning, she advised him to take a battery of admission's tests. Edward charmed her, so when he asked if he could take the tests immediately, the dean made some calls on his behalf. Within the week, Edward had earned superlative scores—high enough to be accepted to any of the Ivy League universities—but he wanted to stay near Tammy. When he returned to the dean, she was surprised that Edward had not applied to other schools but welcomed him to an accelerated program. Still, she had no idea he would graduate with a degree in fewer than two years.

Though he felt badly about leaving Bernice in the big house alone, Edward told her it would be a temporary arrangement while he attended college. She understood. Tammy helped him find a studio apartment near the campus stadium. The apartment, appropriately enough, was number thirteen, and Tammy agreed to move in with him. They needed to make up six years of lost time.

When Edward graduated, he and Tammy moved back to Birmingham into the Rippingtons' home with Bernice, who was not well. The stress of losing her daughter, son-in-law, Edward, and then her husband had weighed heavily on her. She was withering away until Edward's return. Having Edward and Tammy with her gave Bernice a reason to live, but her will alone was not enough. She passed away the next year.

Yet another loss weighed heavily on Edward, so he and Tammy took one month to rest in Panama City at the Rippingtons' beach house, which was now his. The romantic trip made Tammy want to marry Edward immediately, but he insisted that they wait one year. He first had to figure out what he wanted to do with his life.

Tammy could see that Edward was becoming restless, so she gave him the space he needed. All along, Uriel advised him to be patient; the answer would come to him. Hearing from Uriel was like the most precious gift, as it was the first time the spirit guide had contacted Edward since he returned to Earth. Uriel had left him alone to learn and grow.

Edward, feeling somewhat neglected, would have another separation to face. Uriel was letting him know that Edward would soon be on his own permanently. "You are now a man," Uriel said. Before they parted, he added, "You are about to venture into areas that you have only skimmed, but you are prepared. You will live a long, successful life."

Although Uriel was gone, and Edward knew he would miss him, he was excited about the horizons he would reach.

# 21

A sense of remorse came with the loss of Uriel, but as Edward opened his eyes on his birthday, Tammy entered the bedroom with a wrapped gift in her hand. Edward smiled as he put his hand out to accept the package. Before tearing off the paper, Edward reached for two cards Tammy offered. They were funny, which made him smile even more. As Edward opened the present, Tammy told him how proud she was of him and how much she loved him.

Her gift to him was a necklace with a medallion made of pewter. It said "Uriel." The engraving gave Edward chills. Even if Uriel had departed for good, the spirit guide would be positioned next to Edward's heart forever. Edward kissed Tammy and sincerely thanked her for the most meaningful gift he had ever received.

To qualm his restlessness, Edward decided that he would write a book about his time on the planet called Xzanthia, no matter whether readers believed him. With his laptop before him, Edward began typing the title page. The book would be called My Incredible Childhood. Indeed, it was incredible. From there, his words flowed smoothly. After three hours, he had completed several chapters and printed the pages, and then asked Tammy if she'd like go to lunch with him. He wanted her to read his story, but Edward needed to prepare her for the truth about his time away.

While at the restaurant, Edward began to recount his

experiences on Xzanthia. The incredible story was almost too much to take in. For one thing, she was terribly afraid of the idea of aliens on Earth. She had seen several movies about aliens, and they had always terrified her. And those, she thought, were simply fantasy!

Realizing how hard it would be for her to grasp all the news at once, Edward stopped. He decided not to share details about the extraordinary abilities that he had acquired. At the same time, Edward reassured Tammy that he hadn't believed in aliens either, until he'd met them face to face. Though he had previously told Tammy about Uriel, Edward realized that she did not know the full extent of his impact. Even so, she had never questioned his experiences. She believed whatever he told her about his guide; thus, she had given him the necklace inscribed with the spirit's name.

That afternoon, Tammy read the beginning of Edward's manuscript. His words touched her deeply. "This calls for an extra special birthday celebration," she said. She took him out for dinner and had a vanilla cake with chocolate icing waiting for him at home. Of course, the final and most momentous celebration of the night occurred in their bedroom.

ג

For the next few weeks, Edward worked diligently on his book. He envisioned a bestseller followed by hit movie. While recording his story, however, he realized that he needed to reveal those all-important details to Tammy before the rest of the world knew. He had been nervous about her reaction, but she didn't seem surprised when he told her. "Regular people don't go around riding wild dolphins—much less communicating with them!" she said.

Even before Edward's book was published, it was hailed as one of the most outstanding works of the century. It topped the bestseller list, and his opportunities exploded. National talk shows invited Edward to be a guest, and he traveled with Tammy across the country for book-signing appearances.

Stopping in Florida, Edward insisted on spending a few days in St. Petersburg. Edward wanted to swim in the Gulf of Mexico and visit with the dolphins. With that visit, Edward decided it was time to move to the place that he truly loved most. He immediately put his Birmingham house and the Panama City beach cottage up for sale.

# 22

Edward and Tammy found a house on St. Pete Beach that was exactly what they wanted: a two-story home with a balcony off the master bedroom and an expansive wooden patio off the kitchen. Edward turned one of the bedrooms into an office for writing future works.

With all of Edward's success, Tammy wanted to accomplish her own goals. She enrolled in law school with the thought that when she finished in three years, Edward would propose to her. Edward knew what Tammy wanted, and he did, too. Rather than wait, he proposed to her immediately, and Tammy was overjoyed.

Marrying one month before her classes started, they left immediately after for an extended honeymoon in Europe. The moment they landed back in the States, Tammy told Edward that she was pregnant. He was happy but concerned. Edward did not want the baby to start out with the same problems he had. Tammy, however, was more interested in addressing how she would get through law school. They agreed that she would stay home with the baby until kindergarten, when she could complete her degree. Tammy had Edward, and he was what she wanted most of all.

During Tammy's pregnancy, Edward was busy working on his book, and she kept busy with baby preparations. She decorated the nursery for a girl, and they selected Miriam Pearl as their child's name in memory of Edward's mom and dad. Of course, he knew she was a girl! When he eventually sensed that Miriam would be healthy, Edward was ready to celebrate.

Edward had another reason to celebrate as well. He completed his second book, and it, too, landed on the bestseller list. On this book tour, however, Tammy stayed in St. Petersburg. The rave reviews earned him a third book contract, and one month before the baby was born, Edward accepted an offer for a movie deal. Though the pace was hectic, life was going well for Edward.

Miriam Pearl Rippington was born on February thirteenth. Weighing six pounds, eight ounces, she was a nineteen-inch-long beauty with dark-brown hair and greenish eyes. Edward could tell she was bright; she was quite like her daddy.

Edward and Miriam bonded immediately. Edward called her The Peep, which was short for Peepeye. That came about because Edward's nickname was Popeye and he called Tammy Poopeye. They may as well have called her Baby Einstein because Miriam was beginning to say words at only four months of age. Likewise, they could have called her Love Child because Miriam made her parents more in love than they ever dreamed possible.

When little Miriam was six months old, Tammy took her to a photographer. She not only smiled at the camera, but she also turned to Tammy and smiled. She was totally aware of what was happening. When Tammy got the proofs back from the photographer, she showed them to Edward.

Edward immediately noted a blurry image in the proofs that appeared above Miriam's head. It was Uriel! He was there to help Miriam like he had helped Edward. Edward was thrilled. When he pointed out the image to Tammy, she stared in disbelief. Once over the surprise, Tammy smiled. She knew that Miriam was special just like Edward. The dad and daughter were like Siamese twins.

Edward knew what was going on in Miriam's mind, and Miriam, from the day she was born, knew what Edward was thinking.

On Miriam's first birthday, Edward took her into the water, and his dolphin friends swam up to them. Edward then placed Miriam's hand on the dolphin's head. She was smiling. The dolphins were communicating with her just as they had done with him. Edward knew that they were becoming acquainted.

That evening, the Rippingtons celebrated her birthday. Miriam had her very own cupcake and a chocolate birthday cake to share with Edward and Tammy. They were a happy family.

Focused on Miriam's development, Edward wondered when the Xzanthian creatures would want to begin working with his little girl. They existed all over Earth. While they posed as humans and looked normal to most people, Edward was able to see them as they were.

His thoughts of the Xzanthians proved to be a premonition. One month after her first birthday, Edward received a phone call from an advertising agency. The agent told Edward that one of his associates had seen Miriam, and they wanted to use her in a commercial for a natural line of baby food sold nationally. Edward agreed to meet with the advertising executive to discuss the matter.

Edward took Miriam to the agency, where the executive told him about the series of commercials that he wanted to produce. Edward sensed that there was more to the story than the executive was telling him, but he did not detect danger. Edward agreed to let Miriam do the commercials. Besides, she was smiling during the entire meeting. She wanted to be on television.

When they arrived at the television studio, Edward recognized two Xzanthians posing as a producer and a cameraman. They communicated telepathically with Edward that they wanted to take Miriam to Xzanthia to further her learning. Edward refused. While

Edward had benefited from his training on Xzanthia, it was too soon. Miriam was not afraid; she knew that her father would do everything possible to keep her with him.

Edward communicated that he would like to take charge of her training. While the creatures wanted to help Miriam, he was her father. Consequently, when taping began, Edward watched closely. The Xzanthians were using a device that fed information to Miriam. He did not disapprove, but Edward made certain the creatures did not do any more than that.

After the shoot, Edward asked Miriam if she liked doing the commercials. She readily smiled and said, "Yes." Edward then asked Miriam if she would like to go with him when shooting began for the movie for his second book. Again, she smiled and nodded her head in agreement. Edward had decided to keep his baby girl close.

# 23

The movie based on Edward's second book was a blockbuster hit. Though his point of writing was to share the truth about covert government activities, he presented the facts in a fictional format. The benefit was to reveal the facts slowly, giving the public time to become familiar with certain concepts. He did not want to cause panic, riots, or general mayhem.

As his books became part of pop culture, Edward decided to run for political office. He would align himself with concerned citizens, not politicians. For starters, he contacted one dozen people from around the country to aid his initiative to clean up government and the media. His plan, he felt, was essential for keeping the United States from moving closer and closer into an abyss of darkness and evil mind control.

Edward's first step was to run for Governor of Florida. By ending corruption on a state level, he would proceed to the national arena.

For his campaign manager, Edward chose Jim Locksley. Honest and capable, Jim was a direct descendant of Robin of Locksley, also known as Robin Hood. Jim, having inherited the morals passed down his family for hundreds of years, had a deep desire to help the underdog.

Because of his convictions and genuine concern for the people of Florida, Edward was elected in a landslide. Tammy and Miriam were proud of Edward, and they were excited to move with him to Tallahassee. Infatuated with his family, the newspapers wrote glowing stories about the committed wife and beautiful little girl. The media, in general, approved of Edward's platform of cleaning up government corruption, ending street crime, bettering education, ending drug wars, and strengthening family values.

Shortly after the Rippingtons' moved to Tallahassee, Miriam informed Edward that she was pregnant again. Edward pretended to be surprised, but he already knew. He was delighted. On October fifteenth of that year, Tammy gave birth to their second daughter, whom they named Sylvia Eve. Sylvia was a beautiful baby with fine, straight-brown hair and light-green eyes. She had chubby cheeks and an infectious smile. Edward knew that Sylvia was highly intelligent, but she did not have his special abilities.

At the end of Edward's first year in office, he was beginning to see a change in the way politics in Florida were conducted. The shift presented a total realignment with ethics, morals, and honesty. Edward's objective to change politicians back to statesmen was rapidly taking shape.

Edward chose Sam Waters, a former police chief in Panama City, to head a task force to clean up crime as well as rid the state of a corrupt police force. Sam chose Jay Gross as his liaison to work as Waters' assistant. The task force set up units in the major urban areas to shut down drug trafficking and gang violence.

Naturally, it was a slow process. Edward's teams met with plenty of resistance, but their determination began to prevail. Slowly, crime began to drop, and violence diminished. Edward knew, as governor, he had to do more, and he did.

As he traveled the state, Edward spoke with civic groups to emphasize the need for stronger family ties, morals, values, and responsible relationships. Character, he said, began in the home.

In response, he heard resistance and excuses. Raising a family under tough economic conditions was not easy. It took both parents working to provide for their children. Everyone was busy, so quality time with family might be five minutes each day.

Edward returned to Tallahassee with a plan. He would get legislation passed to make it harder to get a marriage license in the state. He spoke out that love was not enough; couples needed to be prepared to raise families before they started having babies. The new law made it mandatory that couples who wanted to get married would have to take a three-month class on the ways to raise a successful family.

Edward hired three experienced psychologists who specialized in relationship counseling to lead the program. The psychologists traveled the state and hired educators to help implement the program. Despite widespread opposition to his idea, Edward held his ground. He led state-wide meetings to help the citizens understand why this program was so important. Once again, people understood what Edward was asking, and they eventually supported him.

Next, Edward began working on a plan to lower unemployment. He had legislation passed that favored new job creation in Florida and solicited new businesses and industries to relocate or expand to Florida. Edward even made a special trip to California to entice movie producers to shoot their films in Florida. He then passed legislation that restricted people from moving to Florida without a job or other means of support. For current residents who were homeless or unemployed, Edward's legislation provided for decent housing and job opportunities. He was determined to make Florida a model state for the rest of the country.

Over the next three years, the State of Florida prospered. Therefore, when Edward ran for a second term as governor, he was reelected overwhelmingly. His beloved family had accompanied him during his state-wide campaign, which gave Edward time with his amazing wife and precious girls, while allowing the people a glimpse of them. Happy to gain the public's favor, Tammy could not contain her pride and love for Edward and their girls, but she made certain that their lives had balance with enough private family time. In his second term as governor, Edward observed that the people of Florida were becoming unified. Strangers would meet on the street and say hello to each other. People were happy, well-educated, and living in comfort. They were not just surviving from paycheck to paycheck, but they were flourishing.

Edward was approached to run for president, but he turned down the offer. He had other goals to accomplish. After his second term ended, Edward planned to travel the country to help other governors make their states as successful as Florida. A few months before his governorship ended, however, he was visited by a group of Xzanthians. They applauded Edward's accomplishments before expressing their desire for Miriam to go to Xzanthia for training. When Edward again refused because she was so young, they revealed that they knew how to care for small children, even babies. Tammy's parents had both spent time on Xzanthia while Florence was pregnant; thus, Tammy had been born on the planet, although she had no memory of those days. Edward suddenly understood the reason why he and Tammy were so close. Even so, Edward was unwilling to relinquish his child to the aliens.

The Xzanthians grew adamant. If Edward did not cooperate, they would take Miriam, Sylvia, and Tammy back to Xzanthia. He ordered them to leave, but as the Xzantians departed, they remarked that they would do what must be done.

Edward decided that he had to tell Tammy. Having no memories of being on Xzanthia, she assured Edward that she would never leave him. Despite her convictions, Edward knew that he had not heard the last of them.

# 24

After the new election, Jim Locksley was sworn in as Florida's new governor. Jim had done a superb job aiding Edward. Edward and Miriam packed up the girls and returned to St. Petersburg. Once back home, Edward began making plans for his cross-country meeting of governors. His first trip would include Georgia, Alabama, and Tennessee. Edward wanted Tammy and the children to go with him, so arrangements were made to accommodate them as well.

The girls, however, both developed colds, so Tammy assured Edward that they would be fine at home during his two-week absence. Though Edward did not feel right about it, he agreed to leave them with extra security. Before he left, he stashed a framed photograph of Tammy, Miriam, and Sylvia in his briefcase.

While away, Edward spoke with Tammy each morning, noon, and night. He told her how much progress he was making. "The governors are all highly responsive to my ideas," he said. She was thrilled to learn of his success.

On his last night before he crawled into bed, Edward called Tammy from Nashville. "I'll be home tomorrow after lunch," he said. Edward was relieved that his girls were safe at home. Maybe he had been wrong about the Xzanthians.

The next morning, Edward phoned Tammy once more before he began a conference call. "I'm about to board the plan from

Nashville," he said. Tammy told him that she and the girls would meet him at Tampa airport. "Don't do that," Edward said. "I've arranged to have limo service." Edward didn't want Tammy to leave their property.

On the way home from the airport, Edward called Tammy again. "I'll be home in less than an hour," he said. Tammy said that they had a surprise waiting for him. When Edward arrived home, however, no one came out to greet him. Unlocking the front door, he was worried. Where were they? Balloons and a "Welcome Home" banner decorated the front hallway, and a chocolate cake was waiting on the dining room table. The only elements missing for a true welcome home party were the most important ones: Tammy, Miriam and Sylvia. Edward knew exactly where they were.

# 25

For the first time in his life, Edward faced a real dilemma. He knew that Miriam would flourish on Xzanthia while being prepared for her future days. Tammy and Sylvia would keep her company while being well cared for. At the same time, he wanted them home. Considering the option of joining them on Xzanthia, Edward had to ask, "Am I being selfish?"

Edward didn't care if he was being selfish. He needed to see his family. Even so, Edward couldn't simply click his heels together to end up there! He needed transportation, but would any of the creatures agree to help him? Suddenly, he remembered a secret he had learned on Xzanthia. Portals existed all over; the creatures used them to go back and forth from Xzanthia to Earth. They served humans as elevators, but the enclosures could also transform to black holes used as transportation highways. The evolution from elevator to portal took place by keying in a special sequential code.

Edward immediately headed downtown to a major bank building. As he approached the elevator, he was stopped by two Xzanthians, posing as security guards. The suited creatures informed Edward that he wasn't allowed to use the elevators. Ignoring them, Edward continued walking towards the portals. The Xzanthians, in turn, blocked his path and escorted Edward out the building. Edward was agitated, but he left the bank to contemplate his next move.

He decided to visit City Hall. The Xzanthians had placed one of their own as an assistant to the mayor, and Edward felt the alien would help him. To a degree, the mayor's assistant said he would help.

The Xzanthians agreed only to schedule intermittent visits, allowing Tammy and the girls to return home every few months to see Edward. Also, the visits would be supervised by an Xzanthian, present during the entire time. Edward was not happy with the arrangement, but at least he could see them.

Sure enough, after Tammy and the girls had been away three months, Edward received a call from one of the Xzanthians, who notified Edward that he would see his family that weekend. The visit would take place at a downtown park on Saturday. The foursome would have a few hours together. The plan did not sit well with Edward, but he determined that a little time with his girls was preferable to nothing.

When Saturday came, Edward left early for the park. As he emerged from his car, he spotted Tammy and the kids standing alongside an Xzanthian. He rushed up to them, but they remained unemotional. Frustrated, sad, and angry, Edward realized that his girls had been hypnotized. In other words, they had been placed in a suspended, non-emotional mental state.

For the next few hours, Edward attempted to bring them around, but all three were robotic. He wanted to lash out at the Xzanthians, but Edward decided to play by the rules. Perhaps it was better this way. He didn't want them to become hysterical when it was time for their return to Xzanthia.

To prevent them from being distressed during and after each visit, Edward said that he would cooperate by putting on a positive face for Tammy and the girls. He would say that he was supportive of their temporary move to Xzanthia if the Xzanthians would not block his loved ones' emotions. The aliens said they would consider his proposal, but the same type of meeting occurred each time they got together. After two years of trying to catch a mere glimpse of their true personalities, Edward gave up. He told the Xzanthians that he preferred to wait for his real girls to return to him.

Attempting to focus on his work, Edward published three more books over the next three years, but his heart wasn't in those projects. Contemplating his next step, he turned into a recluse. At most, he sometimes went out for lunch. Even less frequently, he would go out for dinner, but he always dined alone.

With his spirit waning, Edward planned a trip to Birmingham and visits with old friends. While there, he stopped by his parents' graves. Unable to feel their energy, Edward was confused and disturbed. He desperately needed direction.

He hoped to find answers back in St. Petersburg. As soon as he arrived home, Edward changed into his swimsuit and ran across the sand and into the Gulf of Mexico. Right away, two dolphins swam up beside him. They were the original two dolphins Edward met many years ago.

They informed Edward telepathically that his parents were still alive. No wonder he hadn't anticipated their deaths or felt their spirits! The couple had been forced to fake their deaths to keep Edward safe. Once they had relocated through the Federal Protection Relocation Program, Bernice and Stan felt it would be too disruptive to reenter Edward's life. They currently lived in Iowa, where Paul had moved up from bank teller to vice president. Miriam had worked in a bookstore, where she had first dibs on each of Edward's books.

Edward decided to go see them. He flew into Des Moines and then rented a car to reach their rural town. His first stop was the bookstore, where he saw Miriam. At first, she was nervous, but

Edward assured her that everything was fine. Crying tears of joy and anguish, she let Edward know that she was aware of his family's plight. "I'm so sorry, sweetheart," she said.

After they talked, hugged and cried some more, Miriam told Edward to go see his father; she would spend more time with him later. When Edward entered the bank, Paul nearly fainted. He led Edward into his office, where the two men embraced. They said how much they had missed one another and then tried to cover all that had happened in one another's lives.

Edward wanted his parents to move to St. Petersburg. "I have plenty of money; I'll support you," Edward offered. Paul was uncertain. He and Miriam had made a life in the small town. The excuse was weak. Paul was worried about causing trouble for Edward.

The three agreed to meet for dinner, and Edward had a positive for every negative that Paul and Miriam posed about moving to St. Petersburg. Above all, Edward convinced his parents that their presence would take his mind off his girls, so Paul and Miriam agreed. Edward helped them pack their personal belongings into a rental van, and the three took turns driving to Florida. After three days, their journey ended.

Paul and Miriam were amazed and proud to see Edward's home. They had been affluent, but Edward's wealth was comparable to a king's. Even though their son wanted to share the luxury of his home, Paul and Miriam expressed their preference to live on their own. "We want to pay our own way," they said. Edward tried to argue that a portion of his wealth was from his inheritance, but his parents insisted that whatever money came from their estate was a small token in exchange for all of the grief he had endured. Rather than argue, Edward gave in. However, he said, "You have to agree to accept any gifts I give you."

Within a few weeks, the elder Rippingtons purchased a beach cottage. They made it their own by creating a combination of relaxing and high-energy spaces. Paul also found a job as a legal consultant with the district attorney's office, and Miriam opened a retail bookstore. On the day of the grand opening, Edward held a book signing, and the business quickly gained a loyal clientele.

# 26

Though Paul and Miriam had learned of the girls' transport to Xzanthia, they were hearing for the first time that Edward had spent six years there. They suddenly felt terrible for Bernice, who lost Stan and Edward at about the same time. At times, Paul and Miriam regretted ever entering the Witness Protection Program, but Edward consoled them by saying that they had been remarkable parents, giving up their son so that he could be safe.

When Paul and Miriam were at last settled into the routine of living and working in St. Petersburg, Miriam insisted that Paul have a full physical. Paul felt fine, but he was having a little problem urinating. Knowing that Miriam would worry until he saw a doctor, Paul scheduled an appointment with a physician Edward recommended. That doctor referred Paul to a urologist, who informed Paul that his prostate was enlarged. The urologist ordered some tests and arranged for a follow-up exam.

Rather than return to the office, Paul went directly home. He was too distraught to concentrate on work. Just when he and Miriam were reconnecting with Edward and looking forward to the day when they could meet their grandchildren, Paul's health had to become an issue. The urologist had not told him not to worry, but Paul did not have a good feeling about his prognosis.

He didn't expect to find Miriam home, but she wanted to know how his appointment went. Paul tried to put on a happy face, but she read his mood. "Why don't you take a dip in the gulf? It'll help you relax," she said.

He didn't say it, but Paul decided he may as well enjoy the simple pleasures while he was still living and breathing. He put on his swimsuit and headed directly to the water. Wading to his favorite sandbar made Paul feel better. He shaded his eyes to admire the view of his house on the shore and then turned in the opposite direction to take in the blue horizon. Admiring the beauty of his surroundings, he made peace with whatever happened and felt his body relax. In that state, Paul allowed the current to take him a little further out than usual as he floated on his back.

Absorbed in the gentle sensation of being cradled by the water, Paul didn't notice a giant sea turtle swimming near him. At the same time, being nearsighted, the giant sea turtle somehow decided that the man's leg was a giant shrimp wiggling beneath the water. The turtle swam closer and took a huge bite, and Paul's shin started bleeding profusely. While nearly in shock, Paul began swimming for the shore.

Before he reached the sand, Paul bled out and drifted onto the beach. No person around saw what had happened, but Edward's dolphin friends witnessed the event. They telepathically called for Edward.

Edward came running out to Paul, but he was lying motionless. Edward ran to tell Miriam to call nine-one-one, and then raced back to Paul's lifeless body. Edward suddenly lost control. He ran back to the house and grabbed a large kitchen knife. Miriam shouted that an ambulance was on the way, but Edward replied that they needed a hearse. Paul was dead. Back on the beach, Edward spotted the giant sea turtle in the water, swam out to the creature, and began stabbing it with the kitchen knife. When the turtle was dead, Edward dragged it onto the beach near Paul's body.

The paramedics were just arriving when Edward continued to drag the turtle all the way to his parents' deck. As the paramedics placed Paul's body in the ambulance, Miriam began yelling and crying to see her husband. Edward stopped her. He told her that she needed to let them do their job. He hugged her while she cried in his arms and then made her some tea with a sedative. When she grew drowsy and nodded off on the sofa, Edward covered her with a light cotton shawl and returned to the turtle.

Edward had calmed down by this time, but he proceeded to finish his business. He began removing the animal from its shell and then cut its body into pieces. He placed the chunks into a large garbage bag. That night, Edward and Miriam had turtle soup for dinner. The day had been devastating for them both.

After a private funeral, Paul was buried in a local cemetery. Edward wondered how he and his mother would get past the horrendous event. To his utter surprise, Edward saw Paul's spirit waiting in the driveway when they arrived home after the burial. Edward asked Miriam to go inside; he would be there in a minute.

Approaching his father's ghost, Edward told Paul that he was dead. At first, Paul did not believe him, but after Edward's gentle convincing, Paul walked into the light. He was gone.

# 27

Over the next week, Edward became more and more dejected. Miriam was blaming herself for having suggested that Paul go for a swim. Edward was dealing with the second loss of his father. He was also thinking about his separation from Tammy and his daughters. Edward wanted to deal with the Xzanthians the way he took care of the sea turtle.

As if reading his mind, two of the Xzanthians came to see Edward. They told him that his family was well, but Edward said he wanted Tammy and the girls back. The Xzanthians told Edward that they were taken for a specific reason. When Edward heard that, he grew furious.

"What kind of reason? Are you intentionally keeping us apart to make me suffer?" Edward asked.

Rather than answer him directly, the Xzanthians said that Edward had a higher calling to pursue. His specific purpose on Earth was to bring peace to the planet. Edward had been chosen by the Xzanthians to travel the globe to end wars. In the end, he would rule over Earth. Edward told him that he wasn't Jesus. The Xzanthians told him, no, that he wasn't Jesus. Edward was the messiah.

Edward knew enough about religion to contend that neither the Christians nor the Jews would believe he was the messiah. For one thing, the messiah was supposed to be Jewish, and he wasn't. The Xzanthians acknowledged that belief; they also offered that Edward's ancestors had been Jewish. Even more passionately, they stated that he was one of King David's descendants. It was indeed up to Edward to fulfill his destiny.

Edward stared at them in disbelief. They asked him to look at the birthmark on his upper right arm. As Edward gazed at his arm, the Xzanthians revealed that it was the same birthmark King David bore thousands of years ago. Edward huffed as if they were making up a fantastic story, but he was beginning to realize that they were speaking the truth.

To confirm their words, the Xzanthians presented a scroll that dated back to King David. Some of King David's descendants had left what is now Israel and moved to England some seven hundred years ago. These Israelites were the forefathers of the Rippingtons. The Xzanthians made it clear to Edward that his ancestors had carried the magical powers of King David.

They also told Edward that his mother's family had originated from Israel as well, but they had migrated to England about the same time as Paul's ancestors. The Xzanthians made Edward consider why else would Uriel have been with him. As Edward pondered the news, they said the time had come for him to continue the path to his destiny. Parting, they let Edward know that Uriel would be with him as he fulfilled his calling.

# 28

Wasting no time, the Xzanthians arranged for Edward to fly to Israel. He would take part in a peace negotiation between the Israelis and Palestinians. Edward had never been to the country, but when his plane landed in Tel Aviv, he felt at home there. Uriel told Edward that he should feel at home; in a previous life, Edward had been King David.

Uriel informed Edward that as the new King of the Jews, he had to establish a peace settlement between the two factions. Edward first met with the President of Israel, Shlomo HaCohen. When Edward approached him with the agreement, the president said that the attempt was a waste of time. "Palestinian President Ishmael ibn Azariel wants to wipe Israel off the face of the earth!" he said.

"Forget what you think what the other side might want," Edward said. "Tell me what you desire from the agreement. What is it that you might hope to achieve?"

President HaCohen took a deep breath. "I desire peace throughout the region," he said. "I want to see my grandchildren grow up in a peaceful time without the fear of hatred and anger. I pray for cooperation from the other Arab nations."

Edward spent several hours talking with HaCohen. As the meeting ended, the men shook hands and embraced. HaCohen was astonished by the flow of energy from Edward, who radiated peacefulness. They both knew that something good was going to come from their meeting.

The next day, Edward met with the Palestinian President Ishmael ibn Azriel, who greeted Edward with a warm handshake. Edward reciprocated with a warm hug. Azriel felt the energy that emanated from Edward. During several hours of talks, Edward discussed Azriel's desires to reach a peace agreement. At the end of the meeting, Edward and Azriel shook hands and hugged. Azriel had gained a strong belief in Edward's intent. He trusted that the negotiator truly wanted peace.

On the third day, Edward arranged a meeting between the two leaders. Edward told them, "You cannot overcome your problems. You must outgrow them." The men agreed. After writing down their separate requirements, Edward had the men exchange their lists. In response, both said the other's demands were impossible. Edward then instructed the two men to tear up the papers that they held in their hands, and both did. Puzzled, they awaited Edward's next move.

Edward announced that the two presidents had reached a stalemate; therefore, they would have to exchange leaderships. They looked to Edward for an explanation, so he said they would be less likely to attack each other's people if they knew that they would be killing their own family and friends. When they realized what Edward had in mind, the men said the plan was not an option. If they had a better option, Edward said he was more than willing to listen to them.

"You both desire peace, but if you continue being obstinate, this will never happen," Edward said. "Take some time to tell one another about yourself and your families. After, we will discuss what you truly want for your people." Both parties seemed in agreement: they desired peace.

After their extended meeting, Edward called for a short break.

He hugged each of them and then requested a three-way hug. While they all embraced, Edward generated a loving energy among them. Then they took a twenty-minute break.

When they returned to the table, both men were willing to sign an agreement that would end all fighting. President HaCohen invited Azriel to spend a weekend with him at his beach house in Tel Aviv. Azriel accepted, and. Edward knew that there would be peace.

After the weekend, Edward received a call from the two men, who thanked him for his assistance. Edward continued the meetings with the other Arab countries and the two presidents. Before the joint meeting, Edward met individually with the other rulers to discuss a peace plan.

Each of the separate Arab leaders said that they wanted to wipe Israel off the map. Edward allowed them to speak, but then he said his piece. Before moving on, he ended each meeting by offering a handshake and an energy-changing hug. Though their changes in attitude confused the men, they had lost their lifelong desire to destroy Israel.

The joint meeting included all the Arab leaders and the Israeli President. All parties signed a simple peace treaty, agreeing to stop all fighting in the Middle East. All were sincere in their intentions. At the close of the miraculous session, they also agreed to meet in Jordan to get to know one another on a personal level.

In addition to establishing peace among their countries, they felt a genuine affection for one another. Edward let them know that he expected this to be a lasting peace, and the leaders promised that it would be. For the time being, Edward's work in the Middle East was finished.

# 29

When Edward returned to St. Petersburg, he had more work to accomplish. Miriam had a friend who needed Edward's help. "Thelma Applebaum's son—his name is Albert—is being threatened by criminals who are extorting money from local store owners on St. Pete Beach," Miriam explained. "They are demanding two thousand dollars a month for 'protection,' so the retailers are in a bind. They can't afford to pay the ransom, but they can't afford not to, if you know what I mean."

"Mom, I'd like to help, but this is what the police are here to do."

"The police aren't able to address this problem, Edward. They need you."

Paul agreed to meet with Thelma Applebaum. Though she was in her seventies, Edward could tell that the tall, slender woman had been a beauty queen in her younger days. She was also intelligent and refined. After she explained "the lose-lose" proposition the store owners faced, Edward promised to meet with Albert.

Coincidentally, Edward entered the beachfront store while Albert was being confronted by two tough hoodlums. Clearly, the teens worked for the mob. Pretending not to eavesdrop, Edward overheard Albert promise to pay up.

The hoodlums left, and Edward introduced himself to Albert. "How long have these tough guys been extorting you and the other shop owners?" Albert said that the racket had been going on for a couple of months.

"Have you contacted the police?" asked Edward.

"We tried, but they couldn't help us," said Albert.

The next day, Edward paid a visit to Enrique Domiguez, a former aide to Edward during his time as governor. Upon explaining the problem, Edward asked Enrique what he knew about the situation. "The mobsters are operating out of Ybor City," said Enrique. "That's where their leader, Ralph Malone, runs a nightclub. He has a reputation for being ruthless." Edward asked Enrique to accompany him when he calls on Malone in Ybor City, and the friend agreed.

The next afternoon, Edward and Enrique entered Malone's nightclub. "Where can we find your boss?" Edward asked the bartender. Malone was in his office in the back, so Enrique and Edward headed that way. Enrique knocked on the door, and Malone told him to enter. Recognizing the men, Malone offered them each a comfortable seat.

"What can I do for you, gentlemen?" he asked.

Enrique said they wanted to discuss his business activities. Malone denied any knowledge of the extortion they mentioned, but Enrique plainly stated that the activity needed to be stop immediately. Again, Malone denied any involvement. Enrique and Edward stood, and Enrique said," If you have no knowledge of what has been happening, then you shouldn't mind if we put a stop to it."

Edward then got the idea to enlist the Xzanthians for help. He decided to seek out Sam Chapman, the head Xzanthian in St. Petersburg, because he worked for the district attorney's office and had many connections.

Upon hearing Edward's request, Sam said that he would have several of the Xzanthians pose as store owners. When Malone's men came to collect from them, they would use their powers to cause the hoodlums to forget why they had come in the first place. The creatures would then send them to Xzanthia.

It took only a few days to remove the gangsters from Earth. Before he could understand what was happening, Ralph Malone found himself without an organization. Furious, he began plotting to draft new recruits. Before he could get started, however, Ralph was visited by a group of twelve Xzanthians. The aliens appeared to Malone without disguise, which horrified him.

The frightened gangster opened his desk drawer to retrieve his gun, but the Xzanthians put Malone in a frozen state. While he was immobile, the aliens called a psychiatric hospital to say that Malone was behaving irrationally. They suggested the hospital send an ambulance for the mobster.

The Xzanthians held Malone in a suspended state until the ambulance crew arrived. Malone remained in terror, and once the hospital admitted him, the mobster never wanted to leave.

Though the people of the Tampa Bay area never knew the full story, the store owners were glad their problems were over. They would never be extorted again. Edward had anonymously saved the community.

# 30

Ten years had passed since Edward had seen his family. His beautiful house no longer felt like home. Also, while his initiatives had made an impact, and governors all over the country were slowing initiating improvements, Edward knew that the widespread corruption in the United States government would not end in his lifetime. Like a growing tide of American Jews, he decided to move to Israel. Once there, Edward felt he could build a model nation for the world.

Upon hearing of his decision to move there, President HaCohen said he would be happy to welcome him to Israel. HaCohen set up a meeting between Edward and the Chief Rabbi of Israel, Avram Zvi Weichsel. The rabbi took one look at Edward and knew that he was the Chosen One, the Messiah. HaCohen, meanwhile, offered to initiate arrangements for Edward to be trained for conversion to Judaism, but the Chief Rabbi said the formality would not be necessary. He accepted Edward as the true leader of Israel.

Over the next six months, Jews, Christians, Muslims, and others from all over the world moved to Israel. They wanted to be near Edward. Peace continued among Israel and the other Arab nations; consequently, the Middle East had become a utopia. When Passover came the following year, Edward was ordained the Messiah. President HaCohen was named Governor, and the

Chief Rabbi was appointed Edward's advisor. In addition to all the religious people of various faiths, twelve million Jews on Earth lived in Israel. Miraculously, the country's borders expanded without overtaking any land of the other nations, so the ever-growing populace was easily accommodated.

With his inauguration, Edward changed his name to Ephraim Gdal. Following the custom of others who had moved to Israel, the change reflected his desire to immerse himself in the Israeli culture, much the same as emigrants did in moving to America over the centuries.

After the ceremony, Ephraim made his way home to prepare for the Passover meal. Friends were joining Bernice and him for dinner. As he reflected over the events that occurred since he had served as Governor of Florida, Ephraim Gdal was pleased yet painfully sad that his family was not around to share his transformation. If only they could be returned to him, his life would be complete.

At once, as if his prayer had been answered, the despair lifted; he was truly happy for the first time in years. Realizing why, Ephraim pulled the front door wide open. Waiting in the foyer were Tammy and his daughters. At last, the elegant entrance seemed warm and inviting with a rainbow of balloons and a hand-painted "Welcome Home" sign. Laughing and crying at the same time, the four converged in a huge hug.

From that day forward, they would love and guide one another each step of the way.

The End
Or is it?

Printed in the United States
By Bookmasters